# BROKEN PLAY

BAYLIN CROW

Broken Play by Baylin Crow





Cover Design by Cate Ashwood

Proofread by Kathy Kozakewich

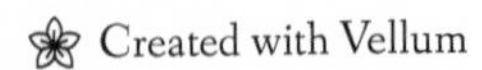

# SERIES NOTE

While there is a real Sugar Land, Texas, the fictional city this book takes place in is simply that: fictional. Each story in the Sugar Land Saints Series will be semi-standalone and each will focus on a new couple. You can read them separately, but I recommend reading them in order. Characters from previous books in the series will make appearances and be referenced while new characters for future books will also be introduced.

To start from the beginning check out Quarterback Sneak (Sugar Land Saints Book One).

Hope you enjoy!

Baylin xo

# ONE
# SHAW

"DAMN, YOU LOOK HOT, SHEPHERD." I settled into the leather bucket seat and closed the car door. The familiar scent of Bishop's cologne mixed with the expensive black upholstery wrapped around me as I looked him over. I couldn't stop myself from leaning over the console toward him. I took his bottom lip between my teeth and tugged. When he growled deep in his throat, I pulled back with a smirk. "You taste good too. I missed you."

"You've been gone almost two weeks, *Wakefield*, and now I'm rock hard. You plan on finishing what you're starting?"

"Nope." I let the word pop on my lips. "We have business to attend to. Daddy's away checking on another club so the son must...whatever. You have to go do your dad's job."

"Then stop being a cock tease." He revved the engine, the sound a refined purr that screamed wealth. He glanced my way. "Belt."

"Yes, sir." I gave him a mock salute then buckled up.

He gently pulled the car out of the dorm parking lot. For all the badass vibes he exuded, he drove like my

Grandma Ginger. I'd told him that once, but he'd shrugged and said my grandma was a smart lady.

"We just need to run in and check things out. My dad said there have been some complaints from customers. The club is understaffed and the manager isn't on top of things. New club, new management, new problems." He sped up as he turned onto the service road. "Shouldn't take over twenty minutes, tops. I just need to talk to him and find out if he needs to be replaced."

"Yeah. While you do that, I'm going to grab a drink." I reached over and turned the radio up, letting the heavy bass thump through the speakers.

He shifted gears smoothly and pulled onto the highway, accelerating and merging into the stream of other cars. I glanced over at him. One large tan hand on the steering wheel, the long fingers of the other wrapped around the shifter. Hands that handled my body so well. I'd missed them over the two weeks of summer break I'd spent with my parents.

Bishop's midnight dark eyes focused on the road while his razor sharp jawline clenched, drawing my gaze to the contours of his face and to his slight cleft chin. His unruly black hair fell across his forehead, covering a faint scar he'd gotten as a kid. He wore a black t-shirt and jeans and smelled amazing. Everything about him was sensual, dark and fucking delicious. And lucky me, I got to enjoy all of it as often as I wanted.

I'd worn a pair of stonewash jeans that had grown soft from many washes and a plain navy shirt and tennis shoes. I hadn't even bothered to fix my hair, opting to toss a ball cap on over my messy, blond hair.

He sat forward and lowered the volume. "Stop staring at me."

"You have something on your face," I lied.

His lip kicked up on the side, slow and reluctant before falling back into line quickly. A twitch. A crack in his armor. I grinned.

"Maybe you should get it."

I leaned toward him again and skimmed my lips over his jaw, pausing for a quick nip, and then traced my tongue along his skin as I made my way to his ear.

"I think I got it," I whispered then settled back in my seat.

He groaned and I watched, satisfied as he released the shifter and moved his hand to his cock, giving it a firm squeeze.

"You're playing with fire," he warned.

I hummed. "You going to burn me?"

His gaze flicked to me, full of promises. "Later. Now, behave. We're almost there."

The highway became busier as the roadways intersected and cars fought to get in the correct lane. It was a drastic difference from visiting my hometown where there was only one stoplight, one convenience store, and instead of having easy access to clubs and bars, we had backroading, tailgate parties and bonfires. Friday nights only meant one thing back home. Football.

Bishop navigated the traffic to the off ramp that led toward downtown. Only a few miles later the buildings began to grow in size and green grass gave way to concrete and metal. Bishop slowed to a crawl as we crossed into the blocks full of clubs, tattoo shops, bars and eclectic shops. The strip was full of bright lights and lines of people that streamed from doorways and down sidewalks. Music thumped. Laughter and chatter came from people out to socialize and let off steam. I watched from my window and took it all in.

Once we passed his dad's newest club, he drove around the building and parked next to the rear exit. The sounds coming from inside were muffled as we climbed out, but when Bishop unlocked the heavy door and swung it open, the full cacophony of sounds was overwhelming.

The door shut with a heavy thud behind us and Bishop re-locked it. We stuck to the edge of the main room to avoid the packed dance floor as I followed him to the bar.

While he circled around the bar and engaged the manager, I pulled up a stool to wait.

Bishop was in his element.

After graduation, he'd become half-owner of the company his dad and mother had built together. Bishop had been groomed for the role straight from the cradle. This new club would be the first one under his watch before he grew the new chain, while his dad would continue to manage the established clubs in many major cities across the US. I knew his mother had passed away when he was twelve but he was tight-lipped on the subject.

While he'd been preparing to take the entertainment business by storm, I'd been laser-focused on football in order to have a shot at a scholarship. Graduating with a degree in journalism and becoming a sports reporter was the dream. I had one foot in the door by making friends with the right people, but it seemed miles away from what the future held in store for Bishop.

I observed the two as I waited for the bartender to notice me. Bishop stood with his arms crossed over his chest and his head cocked to the side. The manager appeared to be in his late thirties, his hair a light shade that was hard to identify under the club's blue-tinted lights. He was rapidly gesturing with his hands, a scowl on his face which quickly dropped. Bishop's lips moved, but the chaotic environment made it impossible to hear what he'd said. I'd bet money he was setting him straight. I chuckled to myself. He wasn't a man who took attitude from anyone.

"What'll you have?" I turned toward the girl behind the bar. Dark hair pulled back in a sleek ponytail, an eyebrow ring and a tired smile greeted me. She must have been new because I didn't recognize her.

I ordered a whiskey and coke, a rare indulgence because I didn't drink often.

She nodded. "Single or double, short or tall?"

"Single short," I replied and glanced back to where I'd last seen Bishop talking to the manager, but no one was there. A heavy glass was placed on a napkin in front of me and stole my attention. "Thank you."

"Starting a tab?" she asked as she tapped the top of the industrial style bar with her nails.

I'd never paid for drinks there before and internally groaned at having to spend part of the meager amount of cash I'd returned to school with.

"Nah." I pulled my wallet from my pocket and handed her a ten. A ten I shouldn't be spending on alcohol of all things. *Shit*.

"Want your change?"

*Yes*. "No." I nodded toward the tip jar. She smiled and slipped the money into a tall fluted jar. "Let me know if you need anything else."

I swiveled around on my seat, one hand holding my glass, and settled my opposite elbow on the bar top behind me. The club was bursting at the seams with people of all shapes and sizes shaking their asses and having a good time. Alcohol burned down my throat and warmth bloomed in my stomach as I nursed my drink. The music was fast paced and my body naturally swayed to the deep bass, tempting me to join in. I peeked at the door marked *Staff Only* where I assumed Bishop had disappeared. Torn between standing there, forced to wait on him, or spend the time dancing, I chewed on my bottom lip. I turned around and attempted to get the bartender's attention again.

She was busy at the other end of the bar and there was no way she could hear me over the deafening noise. I leaned forward, hoping to catch her eye. She glanced over with a cocked brow and pointed toward my drink. I shook my head and waited as she slid a martini glass in front of a girl about my age.

She tightened her ponytail as she made her way to where I stood and placed her hands on the bar, leaning forward. "You don't want another?"

"No, but do you know if Bishop went through there?" I flicked my finger toward the employee door behind the bar.

Her brows furrowed. "Bishop?"

After I introduced myself and explained who he was, her eyes widened. "I'm so sorry. I just started last week and had no idea."

She popped open the register and pulled a ten out and shoved into my hand. I pushed it back at her and reluctantly she returned the money and re-closed the till.

"Jay stepped back and I guess Bishop was with him. I was too busy to pay attention. I wish he'd hurry or at least hire another bartender." She waved her hand toward the customers who were getting impatient and then tucked a loose dark strand of hair behind her ear. "I could use the help here."

A quick scan of the filled stools and people fighting

their way to the front made me feel guilty for pulling her away. "Thanks. I'll get out of your hair."

She gave me a weary smile and sauntered off. I waited another minute before making a decision and whipped out my phone to shoot Bishop a text. *"Come find me when you're done."*

I slipped it back into my pocket, downed the rest of my drink and made my way into the crush of gyrating bodies.

My body moved to the beat and within seconds a soft body pressed against my front. I smiled down at a cute girl with short brown curls. The little dating I did in high school was an experimental mix of both girls and guys and I'd learned that I enjoyed both. But I respected the deal Bishop and I had, so I backed away with a polite grin until we were no longer touching. Not that I minded the exclusive fuck buddy thing he and I had going on. Far from it. He gave me something I hadn't even known I wanted. And during our time together, I hadn't even entertained the idea of anyone else.

As if summoned, or more likely he caught sight of me dancing with someone, a large hand wrapped around my hip. Long fingers splayed over my stomach from behind and pulled me back against a hard chest I knew well. Then we were moving together. The girl's eyes widened as she stared over my shoulder and I imagined that dark gaze piercing hers, claiming me. Bishop was possessive, and while that might not be for everyone, I thrived on it. He was mine and I was his for as long as our arrangement lasted. But we'd never been this open about it before.

His grip tightened and he leaned forward, placing an open-mouthed kiss on my neck. A shiver raced down my spine and I pushed back. He was hard, grinding against me and I forgot about the girl.

He was taking a chance by putting his hands on me in public since he wasn't ready to out himself. Hell, I was taking a chance. Because while I was out back home, I'd zipped my lips quick when I observed the treatment that some of our out teammates received from rival teams.

One of Bishop's hands had moved beneath my shirt, and his warm palm teased my bare skin. I always thought dancing could be sexual but the way he moved against me, I wanted nothing more than for him to rip my pants down and shove his cock in me, riding me hard and deep. Onlookers be damned.

I craned my head around to gauge his expression and found myself staring into a pair of obsidian orbs, locked intently on me. The blue glow enhanced Bishop's sharp features as he gave me a knowing grin and then spun me around. Pressed together from chest to hip, he rolled his in sync with the bass. I gasped as the friction sent pleasure shooting through my veins.

Bishop leaned forward again, holding my gaze for as long as possible before nuzzling my neck. The surprise scrape of his teeth made me moan, the sound swallowed by the loud music. He followed the slight sting with a soft kiss and then pulled away. With his gaze glued to my mouth, he inched forward. The moment his lips touched mine, I froze.

Having his hands on me was enough to trigger whispers, but a kiss noticed by anyone that recognized us would be all over campus within hours. I realized how ridiculous that sounded because if anyone planned to out us we'd already given them more than enough ammo. I couldn't believe we were doing this in public—in his father's club.

A bite on my lower lip broke through my shock and I surrendered to him and parted my lips. He took the invitation and tangled his tongue with mine, all the while rocking our bodies together.

When he backed away, I chased his lips that quirked in amusement. Bishop took my hand and pulled me behind him. We wound through the crowd to the other side of the club where we took the stairs up to the office. On the landing we reached a locked door and he quickly keyed in the code on the electronic pad. Still holding my hand, he pushed it open and led us into a short hallway and closed the door. The shift in lighting was drastic. A dim glow replaced the blue tint and the music faded to a dull roar. I expected to be lured into the office, but he stopped short and backed me against the wall.

Bishop's black hair was a mess of waves and curls and his skin was golden brown under the low light. We were nearly the same height, but where I was lean and toned to stay quick on my feet as I sprinted downfield, he was built for defense—solid, smoking hot muscle.

He let me look my fill as his gaze roamed over me. He moved fast, darting forward and pinning me to the wall with his entire body. Pressed close, he brought his hand to my neck, cradling and rubbing the skin with his thumb as he attacked my lips.

I moaned into his mouth when his other hand crept between our bodies and cupped my bulge. His mouth moved from mine down to my neck where he lightly sucked and licked up to my ear. I needed more and shifted my hips, pressing hard into his hand.

Slipping my hands around his back, I pulled his shirt up and slid my fingers beneath it, scraping my short nails over his skin with just enough force to drive him crazy. The kiss grew more aggressive. When I received that reaction it was difficult not to urge him on, but how far was he willing to take things?

Bishop shifted his hand from my neck and brought it between us to pinch my nipple. I hissed and dipped my fingers into the waistband of his jeans to tease his warm skin beneath the denim. He groaned and rolled his hips.

He reared back and reached for my zipper and roughly lowered it. My jeans and briefs were yanked down to pool around my ankles and my cock sprang free. He licked his lips and groaned. "This is happening now."

His voice was raspy and deep and my body thrummed with need. He gripped my shaft and worked me with skilled tight strokes.

"Here?" My hands went to the wall behind me as he pumped me.

"Don't move," he demanded and dropped to his knees.

The slight worry evaporated when his lips hovered an inch from my tip. I didn't flinch despite the urge to flex my hips. He watched and waited to see if I'd stay put. Satisfied, he rewarded my effort with a wet swipe of his tongue against my tip. It'd been too long without him and I was too sensitive. My eyes rolled back and I held my breath.

"Definitely here." A dark chuckle made its way to my ears as he took the first inch into his mouth and then another. Slow and steady, he swallowed me to the back of his throat, tightened his lips and sucked like a motherfucker as he pulled off then dove forward again.

"Holy shit!" My shout bounced off the walls of the empty hall and spurred him on. He bobbed his head over my length and I couldn't hold back from moving any longer. My hands left the wall to tangle in his hair. "Oh. My. God. Make me come. Please, Bishop, make me fucking come."

He backed away and stood so fast I'd barely registered

what was happening before he spun me around, knocked my ball cap off and jerked my hips back. I'd just braced myself against the wall when he brought his palm down against my ass. The sharp sting turned to blooming heat and sent tingles racing over my skin.

"I have so fucking missed this," he gritted out between his teeth and pulled back.

The sudden loss of his touch was unexpected so I glanced over my shoulder. He held a packet of lube and was coating his fingers before he parted my cheeks. A slick finger traced a line down my crease and stopped to tease my hole.

"Always prepared, aren't you?" My smart mouth earned another hard slap to my other cheek. That was one reason Bishop and I worked so well in bed—and against walls. He was in tune with my body and knew when and how to push my boundaries. I loved that he was big enough to manhandle my large build and enjoyed *punishing* me when he decided I needed it. And fuck, after two weeks I definitely needed it.

"Are you complaining?" His finger sank into me and set all my nerves on fire as pleasure shot through my body.

Moans dripped from my lips and I rested my forehead against the wall as he began stretching me. "Fuck no."

"This will be fast," he warned and added a second digit. "It's been too damn long."

We were so on the same page. "Stop fucking around. I'm ready."

"Almost." He added a third finger. When he seemed satisfied, he pulled out, leaving me empty and aching.

He smacked my bare ass again before the sound of ripping foil sent shivers down my back in anticipation. I spread my legs wider and pushed back.

"So impatient," he whispered and grabbed my hips. "Hold on."

I braced my arms on the wall and he rammed his cock into me with so much force that my knees would have buckled had he not had such a hard grip on me. A grip I was sure would leave marks.

"Yes," I hissed as he drove into me relentlessly. Hard and rough, he gave me exactly what I liked.

I glanced over my shoulder again and caught a glimpse of his face. He stared down to where our bodies connected. His expression, contorted in pleasure, took me back to the first time we'd fucked, watching the sparks of heat in his eyes reflected in the bathroom mirror as he took me from behind. It was a sight I'd never forget. A sight I craved and received every time we were together.

"You and this ass..." He trailed off with a groan as I clamped down around him. With one large hand anchored on my hip, the other whipped around and palmed my cock. Hard and aching with come seeping from the tip, it wasn't going to take much to send me over. I bit my lip to keep from begging him again to finish me off. He liked that too much.

He wrapped his large hand around my shaft and jacked me with quick strokes, timing them just right with his thrusts. I lost the war on keeping my mouth shut and caved. "Please."

He granted my wish and slammed into me hard enough a sign on the wall rattled and nearly fell.

"You close?" he ground out between his teeth

I cried out. "Fuck no, I'm already there."

Bishop's other arm banded around my chest and he jerked me upright with my back against his chest. My head dropped on his shoulder and I came hard, shooting ropes of come on my stomach and coating his hand.

He thrust into me three more times with jerky movements as his release hit. The groan he let loose was so deep I felt the vibration against my back.

We stayed as we were, panting and recovering.

"Well, if that isn't a welcome home from my friend and favorite fuck buddy, I don't know what is." I chuckled and he exhaled hard.

"Keep talking and I'll find another use for that mouth." He pulled out and then led me to the office where we cleaned up in the attached bathroom.

"Are we ready to get out of here?" I asked as he shut off the lights.

He nodded. "Let's go home."

# TWO
# BISHOP

MY HAIR WAS BLOWN BACK by the cooler evening air as we cruised down the highway. I'd left the windows down and played some softer music. Shaw was dozing lightly with a slight smile and contented sighs.

I tapped his leg. "Hey, are you hungry?"

He'd just arrived at his dorm when I'd showed up and probably hadn't had a chance to eat.

His eyes drifted open and he smirked. "For what?"

I felt a rare urge to laugh out loud. "Food and then... whatever else you want."

He chuckled and slouched further into his seat. I hadn't been able to keep my hands off of him long enough to make it home. Taking him at the club probably wasn't my best idea, but when it came to Shaw, I didn't always think clearly.

That was what happened when I had to do without him for fourteen days. And I'd waited for him to come back. Not only was it part of our agreement that neither of us hooked up with anyone else, but Shaw was the only person I wanted.

"I probably should have waited to get you home." I shared my thoughts with him.

"Maybe, but I'm glad you didn't. Besides, you think too much." He shifted in his seat and closed his eyes again. "And no thanks, I can wait on food. Not sure about the other."

Images of all the ways I wanted him raced through my mind. On the bed, in the shower, bent over the couch. Everywhere and in any way. I blinked hard and focused on the road.

Shaw gave me what I craved—control of his body.

*Sometimes.*

I didn't need the bondage and the restraints. I wanted someone who listened without those things. And when he was particularly feisty and disobeying every damned thing I said—which was often—that was fine too, because we both enjoyed it when I spanked his ass. We weren't in a romantic relationship because first, neither of us wanted one, and second, I hadn't come out yet and he wasn't ready to tell the team. My decision to keep it private was mostly because I had a good idea of how my dad would take the news. He was such an asshole, and I didn't trust him with the information.

Though Shaw and I didn't have a typical relationship, he held a part of me that no one else ever had. It was hard to put a name to it. But while Shaw had been visiting his family, I'd had trouble sleeping. I'd paced over the dark hard wood floors of my living room some nights, staring out the huge windows that formed the back wall to the soft lights that lit up the water of my free-form pool. Sometimes, I had silent conversations with the portrait of my mom that hung above the fireplace. With her red hair and dark eyes, she had been beautiful. The only real resemblance we had was the cleft chin she'd passed down to me. On those nights, I liked to think she heard me and understood my restless thoughts better than I did.

Other than the few trips he'd taken home, Shaw was at my house most nights. I'd gotten so used to his presence there that the silence in his absence was palpable. I'd ignored the warning bells that had come with that realization.

If I was being honest with myself, I'd admit I missed him and not just the sex. But I couldn't tell him that because he'd never let me live it down.

I pulled into the driveway of my two-story home. The exterior was made of dove-gray bricks with white trim and had large windows. The black front door matched the wood of the two-car garage in a palette I'd loved since I was a kid and the house had belonged to my grandmother. I pressed the button to open the garage, pulled into the space closest to the door and shook Shaw's shoulder. "We're home. Get your ass up."

"Go away, I'm sleeping." He swatted at the air.

I got out, rounded the car to his side and jerked the door open. If it weren't for his belt, he probably would have fallen out. Of course I wouldn't have let that happen, but judging by the glare he gave me, he didn't know that.

"You're a jerk." He released the belt and climbed out.

"Was I supposed to carry your heavy ass?"

He stretched his arms over his head and yawned. "That would've been the thoughtful thing to do."

I snorted and headed to the back of the car, popped the trunk and grabbed his bag. "You'll have to carry yourself."

"That doesn't even make sense." He hit the button on the wall to close the garage.

He stood aside as I unlocked the door and led him

into the kitchen. We kicked off our shoes on the white tile and I dropped my keys onto the gray speckled granite island.

He yawned again and ran a hand through his shaggy blond hair.

"Still tired?"

"A little." He took his bags from me and crossed the open floor plan space into the living room. "Between the drive home from my parents' and then the club, it's been a long day. But I'm gross and need a shower first."

He ascended the wide stairs, making his way up to my bedroom.

"Just make yourself at home," I called out when he was halfway up.

"Thanks. I will," he said without glancing back but I heard the grin in his voice.

"Smart ass," I growled and then took off after him.

As soon as he heard me hit the first step, he turned and found me charging after him. His eyes opened wide.

"Shit." He laughed and sprinted ahead.

I sped up, taking the stairs two at a time and caught him just as he reached the en-suite bathroom. He spun around and tried to shut me out, not even bothering to conceal the smile spread across his face.

I forced the door open and backed him against the double sink. "Still tired?"

"No, I think I'm awake now." He fingers pressed against my chest and bunched the fabric of my shirt.

I *tsk*ed. "In that case, you wouldn't be trying to be bad on purpose, would you?"

"Never," he said with wide innocent eyes. Eyes that lied. His teeth sank into his juicy bottom lip and my cock jerked.

"Sore?" I asked and he shook his head. I stepped back and crossed my arm. "Take your clothes off."

"Yes, sir." He fumbled with the button on his jeans as if he couldn't figure it out, but ruined the effect when he grinned.

"You really are begging for it. Don't start with the *sir* shit already." My fingers flexed while I deliberated if I'd rather spank him or help him out of his clothes myself. "Clothes. Now."

"I'm fucking trying." He finally yanked down his zipper and jerked his jeans down to his ankles, leaving on his underwear that hugged his bulge and left nothing to imagination. I knew he'd done it on purpose. He liked to be bossed around, but he also liked to be difficult.

His arms crossed over his front as he grabbed the hem of his shirt and dragged it upward, slow and teasing as he exposed his light tan chest and tight pink nipples. Wisps of golden hair dusted his pecs and trailed a thin line from his belly button down before disappearing under his briefs. Shaw had a deep V that I loved to trace with my tongue and I was ready to see it all.

I reached over my head and snagged the top of my shirt and ripped it off. My jeans and underwear hit the floor next. I stepped closer to the shower, reached in and turned on the water, adjusting the temperature until it was hot. The bathroom quickly filled with steam and the mirrors began to fog. When I turned back to him, he was finally naked. His long cock wasn't as thick as mine, but it had a nice curve. I'd enjoyed being on the receiving end a few times, but overall, we both preferred our roles where I pounded his tight hole.

"Get in."

"Always so fucking bossy." He shoved by me with a grin and stepped into the shower.

"Isn't that what you like?" I arched my brow.

"No"—he gave an exaggerated moan—"it's what I *love*."

"Wow." I shook my head. "That was super cheesy. Good thing I think you're sexy as fuck or that would have been a total boner killer."

"Well, you're still hard, so get in the shower before I jerk myself off."

"Look who's being bossy now."

He smirked and reached for the shampoo as I stepped in behind him. I pressed my body flush against his back and grabbed the shampoo bottle from his hands. After I'd squirted some into my hand and returned the bottle to the shelf, I lathered his hair and inhaled the spicy scent.

He moaned again, a real one, and relaxed against me.

"Feel good?"

"So good." He sighed. "I love that smell."

I continued with the massage for another minute before tugging him directly under the spray to rinse, before doing my own hair. We took turns soaping up and while I was focused on his shoulder, he grabbed my hand and pulled it down to his cock, curling his fingers around mine, wrapping them around his shaft.

"Did I say it was time for that?" I squeezed and he bucked into the tight circle.

He gave me a pointed look. "You didn't say it wasn't either. It needs washing too, you know."

I stared at him while I contemplated whether to make him wait. "Bend forward."

He complied with an order for the first time since we'd come home.

"Good." I turned him toward the frosted glass and he used his forearms to brace himself as I made quick work of prepping him. Then I slid my dick inside him in one slick wet entry. My balls drew tight and I bit my bottom lip to stave off the eruption. I'd never get over the way it felt to be buried inside of him bare. One benefit of being exclusive with someone you trusted fully. If it weren't for easy clean up, I'd take his ass raw every time. After we'd been tested, we'd fucked like rabbits for days, and he was the only person I'd ever had that way. It was indescribable.

Slowly, I rocked back and forth, drawing the most vividly erotic sounds from between his lips.

"I love your cock. This feels amazing," he said on a moan.

I hummed in agreement. Between the extra sensitivity, moans, groans and sound of wet skin slapping against skin echoing off the tiles, I wouldn't last long. It felt too damn good. "Jack yourself off."

"Thank fuck." One of his hands left the glass and disappeared from sight, but I knew the moment he started fucking his hand. His ass slammed back against me, driving me harder and further inside him. "I needed this so bad. Too long," he mumbled.

I dug my blunt nails into his ass, the flesh firm with just enough give to sink my fingers into. Sliding in and out, I glanced down and watched my bare cock disappear into him over and over. It was something that always drove me crazy and it sent me crashing over the edge. I slammed in one more time and he cried out as we both came.

Shaw continued stroking as I kept rocking my hips. My eyes closed from the pure pleasure and if I didn't stop I'd be ready to go again.

He winced slightly when I pulled out. "You okay?"

He turned and yanked me by my soaked hair, bringing my lips to his. "So damn okay." And then he forced his tongue into my mouth.

I pulled him in close, pressing our wet, naked bodies together as I kissed him back, loving the texture of his tongue as it played against mine.

When he leaned away, he gave me a dopey smile. "I'm sleepy."

I smirked and grabbed the soap. We quickly took turns washing again and then drying off.

We didn't bother dressing as we climbed into bed and I covered us with the royal blue comforter. He wasn't lying. As soon as his head hit the pillow, his eyes shut and his breathing deepened.

Shaw was perfection. He was hot as hell and we'd had amazing chemistry from the first time we'd hooked up. But relaxed in sleep his features softened. His lips parted slightly and the dusting of freckles across the bridge of his nose which, with the pale blond hair, gave him an angelic appearance.

My last thought before following him to sleep was how Shaw was like an addiction. I wasn't sure when I'd be able to kick the habit.

---

"FUCK, IT'S HOT," Shaw complained as we grabbed our gear bags from my car.

The humidity was stifling as we made our way to the athletic center. Earlier that morning, we'd met up with our conditioning coach and his staff. They'd made us run sprints until we were all exhausted before hitting the weight room and focusing on our upper bodies.

The entire team had been sweating bullets, but that was tame compared to the blazing heat of midday, and it wasn't even close to the worst of summer.

"Stop being a baby. We literally just got out of the car." I followed him up the path to the glass door entrance.

He stopped on a dime as soon as we stepped inside and I smashed into his back. "What the hell, Shaw?"

"I was just enjoying the amazing air conditioning. Jeez, *stop being a baby*." He attempted to mimic my voice, which was apparently low and weird if it sounded anything like the crap that just came out of his mouth.

"You're a pain in my ass, you know that?" I smacked his firm butt hard enough that he reached back and rubbed the spot.

"But you'll still keep me." He peeked over his shoulder and winked.

He was right. I would.

On our way to dress out, we passed a few of our teammates. Nash was already there, along with the newbie quarterback, Memphis, who'd been a walk-on during spring training. He'd been a five-star prospect in high school and accepted an offer in Florida, but after a full year he'd come back to his home state. When Sugar Land got the news, the athletic department jumped on it. Hell, we were all impressed when we saw what he could do on the field.

We had lost our previous starting quarterback, Torin, last season when he graduated. Only a sophomore, the younger player had the potential to fill those shoes. The whole team was counting on the new guy. Talk about pressure following in Torin's footsteps.

We passed by a group of new freshmen who'd be lucky to see any real playing time during the season. Shaw greeted every one of them while I averted my eyes to the large black and gold mural that stretched over a third of the wall next to the weight room. I had no intention of creating ties to people I'd be leaving behind in a year. Shaw, on the other hand, was in a one-man race to see who could be friends with the entire team. Hell, the entire school.

"Would it kill you to talk to people?" he asked as we changed in the locker-room.

"It might and I'm not willing to find out."

He snorted. "Idiot."

I reluctantly grinned to myself as we stepped back on the field.

We tossed the ball around as we waited for everyone to arrive and then it was all business. Playing seven-on-seven, we went over passing drills, while defense countered in the no-tackle mock game. Since afternoon training was player-led, we counted on the offensive and defensive captains to direct us. Along with many of our star players, our defensive captain had graduated the previous year, and I was asked to fill the spot. It was definitely an honor, but I declined for my sake and for the team's.

Two hours later, sweat coated my skin as I made my way to the showers. I stood beneath the spray as the locker-room grew rowdy with football players.

Shaw took the shower next to me and quickly soaped up. When we exited with towels around our waists, he slid into his shorts and casually invited the whole team and their friends to my house to swim. I shot him a glare and he smiled.

"What?" He smiled innocently. "We have tomorrow off and should hang out with the guys. You know, work on your people skills too."

I continued glaring and he continued smiling. *Well, this should be pleasant.*

# THREE
# SHAW

THE SMOOTH RUMBLE of Bishop's car's engine sent a soft vibration through my body as I leaned back. His gaze had been burning a hole in my side since I suggested an impromptu swimming party for the entire team. My lips twitched as I repressed a smile. Getting a reaction from him was like pulling teeth sometimes, but I knew he was silently pissed and that made me giddy as fuck. Giddy enough to think the word *giddy*.

"Pleased with yourself?" he grumbled as he took a turn on the road that lead to his place.

"I don't know what you are talking about." I couldn't hold back my grin.

"It's too bad all these people you invited over are going to throw a wrench in my plans. The things I'd planned to do to you." He groaned and I snapped my gaze to him and watched as his Adam's apple bobbed. "I wanted your ass red from my hand before I fucked the hell out of you, of course after I sucked your cock."

My ass clenched and I had a moment of regret for

inviting everyone over. But it was too late judging by the number of texts continuously pinging from my phone.

"You didn't mention these plans."

"Didn't know I needed to. You were gone for a while and I thought we'd make up for lost time."

"When everyone leaves," I suggested.

"We'll see," he muttered.

"Whatever you say." I'd do something that would make it impossible for him to ignore. I craved the sting that came from his palm right before he slid inside me. The first time it happened there was a long pause after the first smack. After I'd arched my back and lifted my ass, I heard a string of gravelly curses before another blow had landed and fire burned beneath my skin.

A short conversation after and we decided to use each other to give what the other needed. It wasn't pretty but there it was. We'd already been casual friends, as much as he'd allowed anyway. It wasn't easy to get through to him in the beginning, but I'd been drawn to him. I was a people person and had decided he needed a friend. After a while we just became Shaw and Bishop. Even when one of us called it quits, eventually, I knew there would always be *us* in some way.

Thinking of the future made me uneasy so I derailed that train of thought and mimicked his response. "We *will* see."

I'd get my way and we both knew it. Probably.

I was already mentally working out a plan. Yesterday had been quick and rough both times, leaving me aching for more and he damn well knew it. Suddenly I was ready for this get-together to be over. It wasn't even my house despite how often I stayed over and the amount of my belongings that had made the move over the last several months.

We'd barely been able to run upstairs to change before the doorbell rang. On his way to answer the door, Bishop made sure to rub his hand over my ass, reminding me of how I'd messed up. In retaliation I grabbed hold of his red trunks hard enough to hear a small rip and yanked him toward me. I captured his lips in a brutal kiss. His stiff posture relaxed and he pinned me to the wall, one of his favorite things to do. I approved.

"I told you, you shouldn't have invited them. Now stop getting me hard." To prove his point, he pressed his hips to mine and then backed away to adjust himself.

The doorbell rang again. Impatient bastards.

Downstairs, Bishop opened the door and stood aside as the foyer flooded with the guys from the team and chicks in bikinis that were barely covered by shorts and flimsy tops. It was impossible not to look and I could practically feel Bishop's irritation. I wasn't looking because I wanted them, though before him I might have. But it wasn't like I'd tell his moody ass that he was the only one I was interested in. Not just because of our agreement, but just because I liked being with him. He'd freak out, or *I'd* freak out. Some things were better left unsaid.

He didn't swing both ways, but even if I didn't have to worry about girls, he was around other naked men a lot. If I wasn't completely sold on how into me he was sexually, I might be uncomfortable, not that I had a right to. He wasn't interested in them, just like I wasn't interested in these girls. When I was bumped in the shoulder by one of the guys, I shook my head to rid myself of those thoughts

"Dude, you cool?" Logan, one of the o-line guys, asked and I realized he'd asked me another question.

"Yeah, sorry. What's up?"

He lifted a red and white cooler. "Where can I set this?"

"Oh, just take it out to the pool or leave it in the kitchen." I pointed him in the right direction.

"Cool, thanks." He wrapped an arm around his girlfriend's slim waist and they headed toward the kitchen.

Bishop shut the door when the last of the group came inside and I tugged his arm. "Come on, grumpy, let's swim."

To my surprise he went into the ground floor bathroom and grabbed us a couple of bright blue beach towels and followed me outside to the large patio area surrounding the pool. He tossed the towels on a lounger and climbed down the steps into the shallow end. I ran to the side and jumped into the deep end, completely submerging in the clear blue water and swam over to the stairs, taking a seat on the lowest one beside him.

"Oh my god, this feels so good." The sun beat down on my shoulders in contrast to the cold rivulets of water dripping from my hair.

He hummed. "Yes, it will."

"Shut up." I elbowed him. "You always have a dirty mind."

"So do you," he whispered. "And I fucking love it."

I shivered at his suggestive tone and diverted my attention to the party around us before we made a scene. One where I crawled on top of him and stuck my tongue down his throat.

There were already two guys with girls perched on their shoulders, as they engaged in a game of chicken while two other guys set up the volleyball net. People sat around the edge of the pool with their feet dangling in the cold water, while some lounged on chairs and lay out on towels. One girl had monopolized the diving board and was using it for her own personal tanning bed. Two of our teammates were taking advantage of the raised hot tub—though it hadn't been heated since early spring—with girls on their laps and were groping them as if they didn't have an audience. The occasional unsuspecting person was shoved into the pool. Meanwhile, Bishop and I sat on the steps and watched the surrounding chaos.

"Shaw, you playing?" Memphis asked as he tossed the volleyball in the air before catching it again.

He was a good-looking guy with dark hair and blue eyes, tall and lean, as a quarterback should be, and with his shirt off the freckles on his shoulders stood out against his pale skin. He appeared to be the good old boy, hometown type—the complete opposite of Bishop. Good-looking or not, he didn't do it for me.

I turned to Bishop. "You up for it?"

"Nah, go ahead. I'm just going to chill and observe." He leaned back, propping his elbows on the step above.

Not surprised in the least, I rolled my eyes and swam away. "Who's on teams?"

"You're with me." Memphis threw me the ball. "Nash and Logan against us. You're up!"

I smirked at Nash who narrowed those insane yellow-green eyes, made more intense because of his darker coloring. Light brown skin stretched over lean muscle, he was built similar to me and we played the same position. Being rivals came as easy as being teammates.

"Bring it," he said with a curl of his finger and a flash of straight white teeth.

"You asked for it." I served the ball hard.

---

"NICE GAME." Memphis high-fived me and grinned after we'd won by a mile. "You up for another?"

I glanced back just in time to catch the back of Bishop as he disappeared through the sliding back door.

"Maybe later." We slapped palms again before I swam back to the steps, climbed out and dried off as best I could before wrapping the towel around my waist. When I entered the house, I found Bishop in the empty kitchen digging in the sleek stainless steel refrigerator. He closed the door and turned around holding a bottle of water.

I was just about to ask what he was up to when he glared. It took me approximately five seconds to realize the issue. I crossed my arms. "You're jealous."

He scowled. "Why would I be jealous?"

"Exactly what I was wondering. You aren't worried that I'll want to hook up with any of those girls, are you? Or maybe it's one of the guys." I tapped my chin. "No, not just any guy, maybe...Memphis?"

Bishop advanced on me like a hungry predator and I had enough wits to glance around to confirm we were alone before he locked an arm around my waist.

His dark gaze locked with mine. "Do you?"

"Do I what?" I wanted to hear him say it.

He exhaled hard. "Do you want to fuck him?"

"And If I did?" My voice shook slightly because he was super hot when he got jealous, which didn't happen often, and I clamped my lips shut.

Not that I was a psychology major, but it seemed like his way of admitting how much he wanted me to himself. He just didn't know it. Maybe because we weren't in a real relationship, he felt insecure and I wished I could tell him how much he didn't have to worry about that.

With one arm banded around me, the other untied my towel and it dropped to the tiled floor. He brought both hands to my lower back, slipping them into my green swim shorts without hesitation where he grabbed a handful of my ass cheeks in each hand. Kneading, separating and driving me nuts.

"Then our deal would be off." He cocked his head and his eyes darkened, if possible. "You wouldn't bounce on my cock anymore or feel the sting of my hand on your ass."

I groaned as he dug his fingers in. "I knew you were jealous."

"Not being willing to share what's mine doesn't make me jealous." He leaned forward and kissed my neck. "And you two looked awfully cozy."

"I don't belong to you." I gasped as he nipped my sensitive skin and my cock hardened between us. "And we were just playing a game. I'm not interested in him."

"You didn't see the way he was looking at you?" He didn't give me time to respond before he pressed his hips to mine. "And you do. For as long as we are doing this, you belong to me. Your body," he whispered with a slow grind against me. "You."

"You belong to me too." I gasped as he moved.

"Never said I didn't." He rocked against me and I moaned.

My legs shook with the effort it took to stand when he was dry fucking me in the damn kitchen with our entire team and countless others any of which could walk in at anytime. He was growing bolder since I'd come back from break, and I couldn't say I hated it.

The bang of the sliding door made him jerk back and I spun around to the counter to hide my hard on. Thinking quickly, I grabbed a glass from the open-faced cabinet.

"Hey, do you have pain medicine? I think the sun gave me a headache." A girl I recognized from school gave me a small smile.

"Bishop might have something," I tipped my chin toward him and noticed he'd retreated to behind the island. I snickered and his eyes narrowed.

She turned to face him. "Oh, um, do you?"

Instead of answering, he opened a drawer and pulled out a bottle before silently sliding it across the granite to her. She hesitated for only a second before reaching out and snatching the bottle. I suppressed an eye roll at her uneasy appearance. Everyone thought he was some scary guy but they didn't care enough to get to know him. When Bishop's expression remained stoic, she took a step backward, quickly popped the lid and took one before handing the bottle back. *To me.* I smirked and glanced at Bishop whose nostrils flared. It was his own fault.

"Thanks," she mumbled.

"There's water in the fridge if you want one," I offered and glanced down to check my junk and was glad to see evidence of Bishop's attack had gone down. I crossed to the refrigerator and grabbed a bottle of water and handed it out to her.

As she reached and took it, I swore I heard a slight growl and she ran back toward the sliding door. As soon as she was out of earshot, I spun toward Bishop.

"Did you just fucking growl?" I laughed so hard, I had to grab my stomach as I doubled over.

He simply shrugged. "It was funny."

"Your sense of humor is twisted." I calmed down and wiped my eyes.

He took a step in my direction, and I laughed again and raced outside before leaping back into the pool. When I surfaced, I glanced around for him. He leaned in the doorway with his eyes narrowed. I could feel the heat in his gaze no matter how far away he stood and I always knew when he was around. It was like a magnetic pull between us.

Thirty minutes later I was dozing off on a lounger with Nash occupying one next to me and Bishop on my other side. I peered over at Nash. He had a cherry sucker stick hanging from his mouth and looked deep in thought.

Bishop had fallen asleep several minutes before and I'd had to rip my gaze away from his face. He always appeared different, softer even, when relaxed in sleep. I was glad the place was emptying out because it felt wrong for people to see him that way. That was reserved for me and he'd hate it if other people saw the man that I did when they weren't around.

The lounger next to me squeaked as Nash stood and stretched his arms over his head. "I think I'm going to head out too. Tell sleeping beauty thanks for having us over."

"Later man." We bumped fists and he disappeared through the back door.

The last straggler left minutes later, leaving Bishop and me alone. Once the coast was clear, I climbed off my lounge chair and onto his, straddling his shins.

# FOUR
## BISHOP

MY HIPS SHIFTED as warmth engulfed my cock. The wet glide of a skilled tongue stroked my shaft, and a heavy body anchored my legs.

"Shaw," I groaned as I woke, blinking as I became aware of what was happening.

He hummed in response and I glanced down. His green eyes, surrounded with dark lashes, stared up at me. My gaze dipped lower to where my cock disappeared between his plush lips over and over as he bobbed up and down. I tangled my hand in his blond hair and lay my head back down, staring into the sky that glowed orange from the setting sun. I didn't even remember falling asleep, but I'd sure as hell remember waking up.

"Fuck me," I hissed between my teeth when Shaw circled my tip with that dangerous tongue.

He pulled off and jacked me as he cocked a brow. "I'd rather you fuck me."

"That smart mouth of yours..."

"What are you going to do? Make me suck you?" Shaw swooped back down and took me to the back of his throat.

My hips jerked, and his chuckle deep in his chest vibrated down my shaft. *Smart ass.* I grabbed his hair again and pulled hard enough to jerk his head back.

He moaned, sending a sharp bolt of need down my spine. "Fuck, yes. Pull harder."

"I will, but take your ass inside. Bend over the couch and wait for me."

His eyes widened, and his lips parted. He scooted off the lounger and disappeared through the back door.

I stood slowly, taking my time to follow him. I approached him from behind, admiring the way he was already bent over the arm, presenting me with such a sexy picture. "Don't move."

Turning toward the stairs, I took the steps two at a time to my room and gathered what I needed. When I returned, I found Shaw exactly the way I left him. His lightly tanned skin was pulled taut over defined lean muscles, and his legs were parted, giving me an eyeful of his hole and hanging sac.

I stepped behind him and set the supplies on the cushion next to his forearm he was bracing himself with. Unable to resist, I snaked my hand between us and trailed a feather light touch up his inner thigh up to what I wanted. I cupped his sac in my palm, feeling its heavy weight.

"Oh, fuck." He grunted and spread his legs wider.

I hummed. "We'll definitely be fucking."

So much of our relationship was physical, and I loved that Shaw could keep up with me. Sometimes I felt like I was keeping up with him. I'd never connected with someone so in sync with what I wanted. Never trusted someone so thoroughly. I'd never even wanted to. But now that I had it, I couldn't get enough. Months after agreeing to his proposed sexual arrangement, I wasn't even close to through with him.

I rolled his sensitive flesh around in my hand before trailing my finger further up, stopping just before touching his entrance.

He arched his back. "Bishop—"

"So fucking needy, aren't you?" I growled and pressed my other hand against his back. "Stay still."

His legs moved restlessly, making the muscles of his ass contract. I stopped touching him and raised my hand. The crack of my palm against his skin was loud and Shaw gasped, arching his back again as he pushed his ass toward me. The second slap only made him shift harder. It didn't help that he ached for the sting as much as I loved giving it to him. But there was a certain thrill when he purposely disobeyed, or when he couldn't control himself. He was fucking perfect.

My voice lowered. "I said don't move."

He stilled, but I could see the tremor in his legs and knew it wouldn't last. I suited up and coated my cock with lube before slicking my fingers and his hole. I'd barely penetrated him with the first finger before he lost control, rocking back and riding my finger. All thoughts of following orders gone as he mindlessly rolled his hips.

Fuck, he was killing me. I inserted a second finger at the same time I rained down two more smacks onto his reddened skin.

"Stop making me wait and fuck me already!" he demanded and pressed back harder.

"You are absolutely horrible at following instructions, you know that? I shouldn't even give you my cock." Despite my words, I lined up and thrust forward.

His back bowed, and he glared over his shoulder. "Jesus Christ, Bishop. A little warning."

"What do you think the smacks on the ass were?" I set a punishing rhythm. He didn't reply with words. His moans, pants and the way he clawed at the cushions said enough. "You feel so good wrapped around my cock. I fucking love fucking you."

Hell, I loved just being with him. The thought struck me sudden and sharp. Instead of freaking out, I embraced it and got lost in the moment with him.

Skin slapping against skin, filthy words and pleas filled the room as I fucked him like it would be the last time. He pushed back every time I snapped my hips, burying me to the hilt and forcing me to ride him harder. I gripped his hair and jerked him upright with his back to my front as I continued driving into him hard and fast.

"Yes," he hissed and reached up, his hand going behind my neck as he turned his head. With my hand still twisted in his hair, I controlled his movements as I sucked on his bottom lip before giving him the kiss he wanted. He opened his mouth, deepening the connection, massaging his tongue with mine. Shaw kissed like it was his sole mission to devour me. And I'd gladly let him.

"You taste so fucking sweet," I growled against his lips and released his hair.

He leaned his head against my shoulder, and kept his hand on the back of my neck, holding my cheek against his. Panting, he whispered, "You taste like sin."

I chuckled, the sound rough and cracked. I pulled out and walked around the couch, taking a seat and patting my lap. "Ride me."

It was one of his favorite positions, and I slouched low, leaning back, with one hand over my head, and gripped the back of the couch as he mounted me. I held my cock with my other hand and lined up with his entrance.

With his feet planted at my sides, he slowly sank down stretching around me. His jaw dropped in a silent moan that I ate up. He began to rise and fall, using his strong muscled legs to set a steady pace. All the while I watched each of his expressions. Pleasure written in the way his eyes closed and he bit his lip. I wanted that lip so I leaned forward and tugged it free before locking our mouths together.

He stopped moving and the tempo switched on a dime. Fully seated, he kissed me back, forcing me to slow when he slipped his tongue leisurely against mine. No rush, just him and me in a bubble of our own that was impenetrable to the outside world. I brought my arms lower, snaking my hands down his arms, then his sides before settling on his hips. He began a slow rock as we made out like we'd never get enough. Maybe I wouldn't. Shaw was a game changer, and I knew somehow he'd be my downfall.

"I need to come," he said against my lips.

I reached between us and gripped his shaft, working him root to tip. His movements grew unsteady and his ass clamped around me. Our lips stayed touching, breathing each other in and out. My balls tingled letting me know I was close. I nipped his lip. "Come."

His head snapped back, exposing his throat as his release coated our abs and my hand. His ass locked down around my cock, clenching and relaxing, dragging a tortured groan from my chest as I released deep inside him.

We held each other as we recovered, panting hard and covered in a light layer of sweat. I slid from beneath him to his side and brought my mouth to his ear. "Every fucking time it seems better than the last."

The words were spoken softly and he turned his head, eyes full of questions but he nodded. "It does, doesn't it?"

I pecked his lips then I removed the condom and tied it off before standing.

"Come on. Let's go clean up." He stood and I checked him out head to toe. He was covered in come and had a smile on his face. I shook my head because Shaw was unbelievable, perfect in every way, and he was all mine.

He chuckled. "Yes, sir."

Little shit knew I hated that. He smirked and I popped him on the ass as he turned to flee. A smile crept across my face and a lightness filled my chest as I followed him upstairs.

---

WE SLEPT LATE the next morning and then decided another lazy day by the pool was in order, relaxing and enjoying the time off. It wouldn't be long until classes started again and conditioning would move to an ungodly time of the morning, so we were taking advantage of the reprieve.

As the day grew late, we dragged ourselves inside and changed clothes.

"I'm fucking starving." On cue, Shaw's stomach rumbled.

I headed for the drawer that held the takeout menus and pulled them out. "I'll call something in. What are you in the mood for?"

"I'm sick of takeout. Let's get out of the house and go eat."

"Okay, where?" I put the menus away.

"The sandwich shop?" he suggested.

"How about somewhere with a good steak?" A giant hunk of meat sounded much better than the on-campus sandwich shop where we usually met up with the guys.

He rubbed his stomach. "I wish, but I'm running low on cash. Let's go grab some subs or something."

"Nah, I got it. Steak sounds good." I grabbed my keys.

He brought up the money stuff now and then and I knew he wasn't a fan of me spending it on him, but it wasn't a hardship. I had it and we were hungry.

"You sure?" His brows furrowed. "We can just—"

"Don't start." At the door, I slipped on my shoes.

He huffed then grinned. "Okay, if you insist. That sounds amazing." He pulled his phone out and began tapping on the screen. "Let me just invite the guys real quick."

I frowned. Not that I minded hanging out with the guys and he was just doing what we always did—but this time it hadn't even crossed my mind.

He glanced up. "There. Group message sent."

I groaned because *group messages*. "You better not have included me in that."

My phone dinged in my jeans pocket and I glared at Shaw whose smile broadened. "Oops."

"Oops, my ass." I didn't check my phone but pulled it out to switch it to silent before I shoved it back in my pocket. The only person I was interested in hearing from was standing right in front of me. "Was last night not enough? Your ass begging to get warm beneath my palm again?"

His shiver was enough to draw me toward him, but he stepped back. "As tempting as that sounds"—he swallowed hard—"I'm starving."

I jingled my keys. "Let's go then."

Shaw's phone went off several times and he glanced at the screen. "It looks like we're on our own. The guys are...hungover."

"How much did they drink yesterday?"

"I didn't think it was much. They must have done something last night," he said and slipped on his own shoes. "But you were asleep so that's probably why they didn't invite us."

"Well, I for one am disappointed." I adopted a sad expression.

"Shut up." Shaw laughed and shoved my shoulder from behind as we stepped into the garage.

I chuckled, the sound raspy and under-used.

---

THE STEAKHOUSE PARKING lot was full but we'd snagged a spot as a car pulled away.

"Looks like everyone was in the mood for steak," Shaw said as we took the path to the double doors. He pulled the door open and I followed him in.

The woman at the hostess stand smiled and grabbed two menus. "Table for two?"

"Can we just grab a spot at the bar?" Shaw asked.

"Oh, the bar is full. Some big MMA fight with Asher Ramsey, I think. It will probably be awhile before something opens up, but I can add your names to the list if you'd like to wait."

Shaw rubbed his stomach. "Sure, that's—"

"A table is fine," I answered and glanced at Shaw for approval.

He nodded and we were led to a booth. The room glowed with warm tones from hanging chandeliers made of thick wood and candlelit mason jars. There was enough space between the rustic tables to provide some privacy, and wine glasses were set at each place along with folded red cloth napkins. Suddenly the collar of my gray t-shirt felt tight and I slipped my finger inside the material and tugged.

Our waiter approached with two waters in hand. As he set them down, he glanced between the two of us and I wondered what he thought. Because from where I was sitting, it gave the impression that we were on a date. The many times we'd gone out to eat, I'd never once thought of it that way. But rarely did we end up alone and usually sat at the bar or a group table at the burger joint.

The cozy restaurant was by far the most intimate setting we'd been together in public. Other than the stunt we'd pulled at the club, but that had been anything but romantic. *Romantic...* The imagined noose tightened.

"Can I get you started with something to else to drink or an appetizer?" the man asked as he pulled a pad of paper out of his apron.

I shifted in my chair, unable to get comfortable as anxiety sank its claws into me.

"Water for me." Shaw glanced to me, his green eyes lit up like pure bright emeralds from the glowing lights. "Bishop, do you..." His voice trailed off when he glanced up at me. He paused, then turned back to the waiter. "Give us a minute, please."

"Sure," he replied with a smile.

After he'd retreated, Shaw pinned me with a concerned gaze. "What's wrong?"

A drop of sweat rolled down my back. Between the shift in my thoughts about us and the non-date, I felt flustered and confused. *Do they always keep it this warm in here?*

When I hesitated to answer, he kicked me under the table. "Why do you look sick?"

I cleared my throat. He wasn't making it weird. I was. "It's nothing, I'm fine."

Shaw studied my face and then glanced around the table and around the room. He sighed heavily and scooted out of the booth. "Let's just wait for room at the bar. Let me go add our names on the list."

"Sit down." I took a deep breath because even I knew that I was being ridiculous.

He sat and leaned back in the booth. "Well, at least your color is coming back. Dude, what the fuck?"

"I don't know." I glanced at the tabletop and then back at him. "Just had a mini panic attack or something."

"It's not a date, asshole." He laughed. "Chill out."

I growled. "You *really* want your ass spanked."

"Careful. Dinner with the promise of sex after? Sounds awfully like a...date." He snickered.

"Fuck you, Shaw." I threw a napkin at him.

"I'd say buy me dinner first." He made a show of looking around and then smirked. "But it appears you already are."

I kicked him back under the table and he grinned. And just like that, my world righted itself.

The waiter approached again even though I still hadn't scanned the menu. "Have you two decided on something or do you need more time?"

"Actually, is there room at the bar yet?" Shaw asked.

"Oh"—he began to put his paper pad away—"I can check on that for you."

"We'll stay," I said and placed my order.

Shaw wavered, opening and closing his mouth then gave a decisive nod. "Okay then."

After he ordered, he waited until the man disappeared around the corner. “First you want to sit here, then you don’t and now you do?” He cocked a brow. “Geez, whiplash much?”

“I’m hungry. You’re hungry. No reason to wait,” I grumbled.

“Okay, well”—he smiled and tilted his head—“this is nice for our first date.”

“Dammit, Shaw.” I slammed my hands on the table.

He chuckled, appearing damned pleased with himself. “What are we doing after?”

“I don’t know. Home? Movie?” I suggested.

He took a sip of his water. “Sounds good to me.”

---

“GIVE ME THE REMOTE.” Shaw sat at the opposite end of the couch with his hand out.

I held the remote behind me. “Not until you tell me what you are forcing me to watch.”

“Forcing you?” He wiggled his fingers as if that would make me turn it over. “Watching a movie was your idea.”

“So I should get to choose then,” I reasoned.

Shaw shifted onto his knees, doing a weird shuffle across the cushions as he invaded my space and leaned over me trying to reach the remote.

I wrapped my arm around his back and yanked his heavy ass down onto my chest. “Stop.”

He gasped and narrowed his eyes. Before he could open his mouth to complain, I caught his lips in a kiss. A desperate, heat-seeking fusion of two people who couldn’t get enough of each other. I brought my other hand around his back, crushing him against me. His moan was short lived as it turned into a chuckle. I heard the shift of the TV channel.

I opened my eyes as Shaw broke away with a shit-eating grin and held up his prize. He'd relieved me of the damn remote with his distracting tongue.

Shaw didn't move back to his side of the couch, deciding to sidle up against me and pulled the blanket from the back of the couch. He draped it over himself and then casually threw half to me. My gaze swung from him to the blanket and back. It wasn't the first time we'd sort of cuddled, but usually sex of some sort was involved whether beginning or ending. *Not* to watch a movie.

Shaw settled on a movie and relaxed. He gave me the side-eye. "You're staring again."

# FIVE
# SHAW

"I'M DECIDING what to do with you." Bishop's gaze sent a wave of heat through my body.

"Well, whatever it is, it'll have to wait. I've been dying to see this." I snuggled further into his fluffy ass couch. It was like melting into a cloud. A cloud with a fierce thunderstorm sitting right next to me.

I knew he was debating on whether to push me away, especially after the situation at dinner. Lately it had given me a little rush to tug him out of his comfort zone.

When he slouched next to me, I mentally fist pumped. It always seemed like it was a game of who could get the upper hand.

"Why are you smiling?" His gruff voice held a note of irritation.

"Why aren't you looking at the screen?" I deflected.

Instead of answering my question, the cushion dipped as he adjusted himself. Peeking out of the corner of my eye, I noted his attention was on the sixty-five inch flat-screen as the movie came on.

Every minute that passed, we sank heavier against each

other. It surprised me how comfortable he seemed with it as he leaned against me, but then a small snore startled me just as a quiet scene in the movie played out. I glanced over and saw he'd fallen asleep with his head tipped back against the cushion. I chuckled when he shifted and used my shoulder as a pillow.

He was a heavy sleeper and would get a crick in his neck if he didn't lie down, so I stood and urged him down onto his back and adjusted his heavy legs so he could stretch out. The couch was oversized but not quite enough room for both of us, so I decided I'd finish the movie from the recliner and then try to wake him to go upstairs. Or at least that was the plan.

I laid the blanket over him but when I was pulling away, his hand shot out and wrapped around my forearm. He dragged me down half on the couch and half on him. After an awkward fight with the blanket, he managed to wiggle it free and spread it over both of us. He did all of this with his eyes closed. I chuckled, my chest shaking on top of his.

"Mmmm," he hummed against my neck. His breathing deepened again and wisps of air tickled my skin as he slept.

I attempted to get up but his arms banded tighter around me. The little resistance I had fled as I relaxed against him. He hummed again in what sounded like contentment and I lay there listening to his light snores and soaking up the warmth of his body. I wanted to kiss him again. I wanted to kiss him forever.

The last thought caught me off guard and I froze against him.

He grunted. "Go the fuck to sleep, Shaw. Stop waking me up."

I snickered again despite the churning in my stomach. There was no way I was sleeping soon and under no circumstances could I ever tell him about the asinine thought that had crossed my mind. The longer I lay there and obsessed over it, the more I realized it was true. I wanted to be more than just an arrangement to Bishop.

How would he react if I told him? He'd probably end things and I wasn't ready for that. Not yet. I had to keep my mouth shut.

---

THE BALL SAILED through the air and into my hands, a beautiful pass from our new star quarterback, Memphis. I turned and bolted toward the end zone. I didn't have to glance back to know Bishop had taken off in an all-out sprint behind me.

The hunter closing in on his prey, I thought with a grin.

Only Bishop would thrive the way he did with us being on opposing sides of the field. I was a wide receiver and he was a safety on defense, and since no one else on the team could keep up with me, Bishop and I were often matched man-on-man.

His singular focus on catching my ass drove my own as I kicked my legs up higher, cleats digging into the turf, as I tried to stay ahead of him. But I could hear him hot on my tail and breathing down my neck. My legs were suddenly wrapped up when he dove for me and a grunt whooshed out of me as I hit the ground. I rolled onto my back and glanced over to where he lay next to me. He gave me a satisfied grin and I scowled. *Fucker.*

"Took you long enough," I taunted as I sat up, checking my elbows for turf-burn.

"Well, if you were faster, I wouldn't have caught you at all," he responded, like a prick, as he also sat up.

"What the fuck, guys?" Nash marched over to where we sat panting on the ground. He ripped off his helmet and rubbed his temples. "This isn't a real game. Touch only. You weren't supposed to tackle him for fuck's sake, Bishop. You two can't just do whatever you want all the time."

Bishop and I knew the score. If he hadn't taken me out, I'd have had the upper hand and we couldn't have that, could we? I secretly loved the power games between us. Getting chewed out by the team was a necessary evil.

"My bad." Bishop rose to his feet and Nash rolled his eyes.

"You're not sorry. I don't even know why I bother."

"Me neither," Bishop's rough voice came from behind me.

Nash who'd been walking away spun around. "Did you say something, demon boy?"

I burst out laughing as I stood and received a death glare from Bishop.

He shoved the ball in Nash's hands. "I'd repeat myself but I'm sure you caught it the first time."

"You're such an asshole," Nash said as he headed back to where the team waited.

"Sorry, guys," I said as we approached them.

The new quarterback's gaze bounced between Bishop and me.

"Don't even try to figure out their bullshit." Nash's annoyance was clear.

"Stop being such a dick," I whispered to Bishop.

He frowned. "All I said was I didn't know why he bothered."

"I don't know why I like you." I bumped his shoulder with mine.

"Me neither," he agreed with a rare self-deprecating

tone. Now and then an unexpected comment like that would slip out and I wanted to dig further. But somehow I knew that if I did, he'd shut me out.

"It was a joke," I muttered.

"You two can sit out." I realized Memphis was talking to me and Bishop. *What the fuck?*

The thing about summer conditioning was that while our conditioning coach called the shots in the early morning, the team got together without Coach for unofficial training in the afternoons several days a week. The latter were player-led, which meant that unless we wanted to seriously rock the boat, we listened to the captains of both offense and defense.

Well, looked like the newbie, Memphis, was stepping up.

I glanced at Bishop. "Dude, I think we just got benched."

His lip twitched and he saluted Memphis who didn't look like he appreciated the gesture.

"No problem," I said for both of us.

"Maybe when you two get your heads back in the game..." he trailed off with a meaningful stare.

It was never fun to be sidelined, but I respected that he was looking out for the team like any good captain would. He hadn't earned the official title yet, but it was a foregone conclusion Coach would make him starting quarterback in the fall.

"Understood," I answered.

As we walked off the field we both took our helmets off and then sat on a bench together. Sweat dripped down my temples and the back of my neck. My jersey stuck to my body like a second skin and I lifted the material, trying to gain some relief. Even indoors I couldn't escape the Texas heat.

"You're such a troublemaker," Bishop said.

When I jerked my head toward him, his lips twitched.

"Whatever, *demon boy*. You were the one who chased me down." I laughed and he shoved my shoulder. "We should be wrapping up soon anyway. What are we doing after?"

"I agreed to dinner at my dad's." Bishop lips fell into a flat line.

"Oh, okay. Well, I hope everything's okay." I wanted to ask what was wrong, but didn't want to feel the sting of rejection if he shut me out.

Bishop didn't discuss his relationship with his father much but when he did, it was obvious there was some animosity there. Knowing that after graduation he would to take over half of the company made me wonder how that would work. Maybe they'd have a better working relationship than their strained personal one.

"Business." He sighed. "It's always business, so I'm sure it's about the new club. He just said we needed to talk. I don't have a choice or I'd definitely skip."

So much for the working relationship.

"Well that sounds boring as fuck. I'll just stay at my place tonight."

The deep growly thing he did when he disapproved made an appearance. "What if I want to do dirty things to you tonight?"

"Then I guess you'll enjoy your hand while thinking about me," I quipped and received a rare raspy chuckle.

"Or you could come over after?"

"Oh, I could, huh?" I cocked a brow. "How bad do you want it?"

"I think you know how bad but if you need a demonstration, we can take this elsewhere."

"Bad enough to beg?" I continued to tease him.

"Never. But you—" His deep voice lowered and his gaze dropped to my lips that parted under his scrutiny. "I love it when you fucking beg."

My skin erupted in goosebumps, but I adopted a blasé tone. "We'll see."

Bishop smirked. "Let's get back out there. We're just getting into more trouble over here."

---

MY ROOMMATE WOULDN'T SHOW up until the fall semester started, so my dorm room was empty when I arrived.

I dumped my gear bag by the plain dark wood desk and set my keys and wallet on the matching bedside table. After digging in the mini-fridge for a bottle of water, I kicked back on the worn gray comforter that covered my bed, leaned against the headboard and crossed my ankles. I took a drink and set the bottle aside before I pulled up my parents' contact info on my phone and hit video.

My face showed up in a window on the screen, bright green eyes, a sprinkle of freckles dotting the bridge of my nose and a dusting of stubble on my square jaw that framed my full lips. I ran my hands through my hair, still damp from the shower, ruffling it as I waited for my mom to pick up.

Seconds later my mother's face came into view. Sarah Wakefield, my younger brother and I shared the same blond hair, though hers was long, streaked with white and parted in the middle. Her green eyes were a shade lighter than ours but the resemblance was clear. Small wrinkles at the corners of her eyes deepened as she beamed. "Hi, sweet boy. I miss you so much already."

I could barely hold back the eye roll, but I grinned at the pet name my mother persisted in using.

"Not sure 'sweet boy' has ever fit me."

She gasped as if surprised. My mom was a bit naïve and one of the sweetest women in the world. She never had a bad word to say about anyone. She saw the good, ignored the bad and tended to be sentimental. I didn't think I'd ever escape my childhood nickname.

*Sweet boy*. I cringed. *Never let Bishop hear that shit.*

"How are you, Mom?"

"Better now that you've called. You were only home a short time, but it was nice and now I miss my boy." Her grin faltered. "I just wish we'd been able to do more for you. Then we'd be able to spend more time together during the summer and holidays."

I loved visiting home. The three bedroom, one bathroom home was small, but smelled of whatever goodies my mom happened to be baking. Pictures of our family hung on the walls and with magnets on the refrigerator. And every piece of furniture had a memory attached to it.

"You and Dad do plenty. Not everything is about money, Mom." I smiled. "And besides, I love playing football."

It was true. Football had been the one thing I was genuinely good at. When I'd been scouted by several colleges and then received a full-ride athletic scholarship because of my high school stats, I'd damn near cried. My mother *had* shed a tear—or many. I chuckled at the memory.

"Oh, I know. We're so proud of both you and your

brother. I lucked out with you two." She sniffed and her eyes welled up.

Rendon had received an academic scholarship, the smart little shit, and he'd be beginning his first semester at Sugar Land in the fall. Sometimes he was a pain in my ass, but he meant the world to me.

"Thanks, Mom." The smile I received in return lit up the screen. "Where's Dad?"

"Out in the garage fussing with his car last I saw him. Hold on a second."

I heard the tapping of her shoes as she went to find him. "Phil, honey, Shaw is on the phone."

"Bring it here, babe. My hands are covered in grease."

The screen shifted and I glimpsed the inside of the one-car garage and the wall my dad used to organize all of his tools before slanting downward to my father. He was crouched next to his car and wiping his hands with an old T-shirt rag.

"I'll hold it. You just talk," my mom said.

He glanced at the screen and held up his messy hands and I noticed that his gray hair was mussed as usual.

"The car's giving me trouble again," he explained and shook his head.

"It is fixable?" I frowned.

"Of course it is." He waved me off and his blue eyes grew serious as he prepared to launch into details about the issue. One day I'd stop taking the bait, I promised myself. He loved to work on cars and he loved to talk about cars.

That was one area in which I did not excel and lucked out with him as a dad because my old beater had constantly needed work.

"Honey," my mother cut in and cleared her throat.

"Oh, right, I'm not going to make your mom hold the

phone while I spout off about the car. You boys out of training early today?"

I chuckled because he tended to lose track of time when tinkering around in the garage. "It's getting pretty late."

"Oh, I didn't realize how long I'd been out here. Well, how's everything going?"

"Good, just conditioning and killing time, mostly. We start summer classes next week but it'll be slow." Summer term was boring. The campus was dead but some athletes used it to cut back how many classes they had to take in the fall. That was my plan and part of my scholarship. "Where's Rendon?"

"Hanging out with a friend, I guess, like every other night this week. Boy graduates and now he's never home." He sighed with exasperation.

I remembered what I'd been doing after graduating so I wasn't surprised. My parents would not have approved. "I'll try him on his phone then."

"You keep an eye out for your brother once he's out there." He waited for me to agree.

"I promise." Rendon and I had both resembled our mom in many ways, but only I had inherited my dad's six-two height and lean strength. Still, Rendon was a good-looking kid and I'd have my hands full, no doubt. "All right, I just wanted to check in. Love you guys."

"Love you too. Smoke is starting to come out of your momma's ears so I'm going to say goodbye before she gets upset." She gasped and my dad winked.

Mom's face came back into view. "You know better than to listen to him. I love you more, sweet boy. Take care and don't forget to call your grandma."

"I will." I hit end and pulled up my grandma's number.

## SIX
## BISHOP

MY DAD'S house was as pretentious as its owner. I scowled as I pulled around the circular stone driveway that wrapped around a large tiered fountain. I'd once thought the centerpiece was perfect when my mother's favorite flowers had bloomed in a kaleidoscope of colors each spring. After my mother passed, my father replaced them. The impersonal greenery—without a twig or bloom out of place—seemed as superficial as the man who fathered me.

Though admittedly I appreciated nice things, he was obsessed with obscene extravagance.

I parked my car close to the doors and stormed up the steps to the massive porch that boasted large white pillars and oversized double doors made of exotic wood and let myself in without knocking. Knowing I'd find him in his office, because he rarely left it when he was home, I crossed the foyer and headed straight for it. I passed through the hall where expensive artwork hung in the place of family portraits that my father had removed after my mother died. There were no pictures of *any* of us. The place was like a museum instead of a home.

The unmistakable smell of my dad's favorite expensive Cuban cigars wafted through the air, the scent growing stronger as I approached. He was seated in an English-style leather chair.

"Dad," I announced myself as I stopped at the threshold of the room.

His gaze slowly lifted, eyeing me head to toe. I was wearing a pair of dark jeans and a navy t-shirt. Nothing special, but the slight curl of his lips showed his disapproval.

"Did you not have something more appropriate to wear?" He placed his half-smoked cigar in the ashtray, letting it burn itself out.

I glanced down at my clothes wondering what the issue was. "Appropriate for what exactly? Thought we were just talking over dinner."

He rolled his chair back and stood to his full height, equal to mine. Hell, we looked so similar I might as well have been staring at myself thirty years in the future. "Yes, well we have dinner guests arriving soon."

"Guests," I deadpanned. "Well, had I known, maybe I'd have worn something else, but since you failed to mention it, this is what you get. Who's coming?"

"That's what we need to talk about." He rounded the desk and then leaned back against it, crossing his legs and folding his arms over this chest. "It's come to my attention that my son and heir is engaging in unacceptable behavior."

"What do you mean?" I furrowed my brow and stepped into the room.

"This boy, Shaw Wakefield." Disdain twisted his features. "Who is he to you?"

I tensed. "Why are you asking about Shaw?

"Don't ignore the question."

"He is none of your business," I snapped.

"He wasn't. You're right, but now that my son is in a relationship with him, he is."

The statement was made so casually, I was caught off guard and warning bells sounded in my head. "How do you even know what I'm doing?"

"You weren't exactly discreet when you fucked him in the club. Did you know the alarm company is so kind as to send me notifications for when the access code to the offices is used? You can probably imagine my surprise when the security camera caught something I'd hoped to never see." He squeezed his eyes closed and then pinned me with a disapproving look. "So I made inquiries about him."

"Inquiries?" I repeated in a flat tone. My dad was asking around about Shaw. The invasion of not only mine, but Shaw's privacy made my blood boil.

"Let's cut to the chase. I have been aware of the boy for months, but I saw no hint that you intended to go public with him, so I left it alone. I didn't dig or even know his full name. I trusted you and thought you were old enough —*smart enough*—this time to navigate that yourself. But I've been proven wrong and now you pose a risk to the future of the company. I can't sit back and watch as you tarnish my name."

My brow furrowed as I sorted through what he'd said. It didn't make sense and I had so many questions. "How have you known about Shaw for months if you just saw the video? What do you mean *this time*? And how am I tarnishing your name exactly?"

"There's not much I don't know when I make it my business to know." He gave me a pointed look. "You have a relationship with a boy that doesn't have a dollar to his name. He's a nobody, Bishop, and he's already sunk his claws into you. What were you thinking?"

I stepped forward and lowered my voice. "I was thinking it's none of your damn business."

"Then you should have kept that part of your life private, boy. He never stays in his dorm, opting to stay at your home almost every night. It's easy to conclude you spend too much time with him. And I'm under no illusion as to what you two do under that roof. And even if I were, the video dispelled that belief. It must be nice for him. Getting under the skin of a rich boy like yourself."

"You checked his dorm? What the fuck?" The man had no sense of boundaries. I was almost at a loss for words. "Did you have someone tailing me too?"

"No need for that. People are happy enough to answer questions with the right compensation."

"Unbelievable," I muttered while rubbing the bridge of my nose. The whole thing was ridiculous.

"Believe it," he said with a bored tone. "It was easy enough to find out who he was. And then after discovering he is on a full-ride scholarship, I dug deeper. The boy is poor, comes from a low income family and is not a suitable partner."

"Stop calling us boys! And you have stepped so far over the line it's sickening."

"Watch your tone. If you'd act like a man, you'd be addressed as one. You'd risk your fortune for some hard-up college kid looking for a free ride?"

I couldn't stop shaking my head. When I'd agreed to come for dinner I'd had no clue what waited for me.

"I've found a solution for this whole mess." He waited for me to respond, but I was rendered mute. "You'll marry Mya Vance."

My spine went rigid. "Well, that escalated quickly.

Might I ask why finding out I'm gay led to marriage...to a woman? One I don't even give a shit about?"

"I'm not *just* finding out you're gay, Bishop." He sighed. "You haven't given me much choice and believe it or not, it wasn't a decision I made lightly."

He glanced at his watch as if I was taking up his valuable time.

"Your decision?" I took a step back as I narrowed my eyes. "Why would I marry her? You can't force me to do something like that."

"Wrong." His nostrils flared. "Now that I've discovered how gullible my son is, I've decided to step in and fix this mess. The Vances have wanted to merge their high-end bar chain with my clubs for years and I've always set the idea on the back-burner. I spoke to her father and this whole predicament is fixed. You'll marry Mya. You only have yourself and your irresponsible behavior to blame."

I reared back. "Excuse me?"

"I didn't stutter, boy. You'll put an end to your relationship and marry the Vance girl. She comes from a wealthy family and the business will profit from the merger." He nodded to himself.

I laughed at the sheer amount of bullshit in the room but it wasn't funny at all. I was livid.

"What about the fact that I prefer men?"

"What about it?" His expressionless question made me want to shake him. He couldn't be serious.

"If I found a rich man to marry, would that be okay?" The pointless question was asked to make him say it and admit the real issue.

His lips thinned. His jaw tightened. "I'm not sure how you could continue the family line with a man."

I gaped at him.

"And I don't care how it happens," he powered on. "Even if it's artificial insemination. But before I go I want to see a grandchild with my blood and the last name Shepherd."

"One, you're out of your mind. And two, once the company is part mine, you can't take it away." I pointed out.

"Maybe," he agreed but his gaze sharpened. "I guess then the smart thing to do would be to not make it official until you do produce your own son."

"You've officially lost it!" He'd gotten progressively worst since my mom died. Hell, he didn't even date. *Too many greedy leeches* he'd explained. "Let me get this straight. *Now*, I have to get married and have my wife pop out however many babies it takes to have a boy and *then*, I'll become part owner?"

I was panicking and he was cool as a damn cucumber.

"Let me ask you something." He cocked a brow. "If I asked you to break things off with Shaw Wakefield and I'd have no issue with you marrying a rich man, what would your response be?"

What *would* my response be? Marrying a rich man, any man, felt like cheating on Shaw. Even though we weren't together in the traditional sense, it felt wrong. The hard truth of how I felt about Shaw was being shoved in my face and I had no choice but to face it under the circumstances. The thought of marrying someone else, having to end things with Shaw, made me ill.

When I didn't respond, he pointed at me.

"You see? This is why. You're in too deep with him. Has it ever occurred to you than when he looks at you all he sees are giant dollar signs? That he's after your money?"

"You don't know him."

"I know his type and I've worked too hard for you to

throw it away on some plaything. You're fooling yourself if you think for a moment it's more than that for him."

"He's not a plaything." I banged my fist against the wall.

He huffed. "That is exactly the issue. That right there is why I will secure the company's assets at whatever cost. You are emotionally invested with someone beneath you. Consent and let's get this over with."

"Let's get this over with," I echoed. "A marriage. A lifetime commitment. You really are a lousy motherfucker."

His gaze bore into mine. "You care about him and he's using you."

"So you keep telling me. Where is this coming from? Mom never did those things to you."

"No, she didn't and that's why. She had plenty of her own money. A perfect example of why that boy has to go."

I saw red. "It's your fault she's dead!"

He was in my face before I could blink. His hand was raised and shaking. It took me a moment to realize he'd intended to hit me and I hoped like hell my mother wasn't witnessing any of this. For whatever reason, he calmed and stepped away.

He smoothed his shirt. "You don't know what you're talking about so do not speak of her again. Your mother understood money, so don't tell me what she'd do. Gabby is not here, Bishop. Do not bring her into it again." His voice cracked on the last word, the only chink in the man's heart of cold steel.

I gathered my composure. "Ignoring it doesn't change the facts. Business before family."

He took a step forward but stopped. "Watch yourself, Bishop."

"This was her business too and she always meant it to be passed on to me. Gabrielle Shepherd was many things, everything to me really, but a conniving backstabber was not one of them." My face heated in anger.

"Let me educate you on settling with someone beneath you. Another woman came before her and almost wiped out my bank account, including the inheritance I had from my parents. After a long drawn-out process she was ordered to return the money. I learned a lesson from her. I won't allow the same to happen to you, although I'd think you'd have learned it from that kid. What was his name? Kyle?"

Kyle had been a friend of sorts. In high school we'd used each other to explore and experiment with what we both knew was true. We were gay. Then one day my dad almost caught us and it sent Kyle running scared. He avoided me at all costs in the hallways. It wasn't a big deal or a surprise. And I had no inclination to think of him again.

He wasn't Shaw.

"What do you mean I should have learned my lesson?"

He tossed his head back with a laugh. "Surely you are not that naive. Everyone has a price and his wasn't even that high. He accepted the offer in less than a minute. A minute, Bishop. Open your eyes."

Stunned, I could only stare back. "To clarify, you paid him not to hang out with me?"

"I paid him because you weren't nearly as sneaky as you thought you were. Turns out not much has changed. Though I admit I'd hoped it was a temporary lapse in judgment back then. Clearly I was wrong."

"You paid him to..."

He waved me off. "I think I've proved my point enough."

My hands clamped together until my knuckles turned white. I hadn't had feelings for the guy but my dad had still managed to surprise me. Judging by the slight tilt of his lips, he was quite pleased at my reaction.

Shaw was different. Not a question in my mind. "If you've known about Shaw, why didn't you try to bribe him also?"

"I feel like this conversation is going in circles. You have been discreet with him up until this point. I thought with age you'd learn to keep certain things in the dark where they belong. Certain freedoms are not afforded to people of means."

"Oh my god, get with the fucking times. This isn't about money at all. Or maybe it is, but the biggest issue is that I'm gay and now you're worried the whole world will find out." All this talk and that was the heart of his objection.

"You'll marry Mya. That's the end of it." He turned his back as if the conversation was over and decided.

"No, it's fucking not. Why in your twisted mind do I have to marry at all?"

"Because you're being reckless. You think it's not written all over your face how you feel about that kid?" He turned back around and pointed at my face. "I'm not going to allow this train wreck."

"Forcing me to marry would be the train wreck," I gritted through my teeth.

"Believe me, refusing would be worse. I've promised the Vances. Mya's father agrees that tying our families together along with the merger is just smart business and it saves me from the consequences of you making a disastrous decision, left to your own devices. If you don't follow through, I will remove your position as part owner next year."

"First, you bring someone else into the company and now... You wouldn't do that," I insisted. "It was Mom's company too."

"Do *not* bring her into this. She and Mya's mother planned your marriage since you two were in cradles."

That was true but only out of fun. She'd never have asked me to do this.

"Be smart, Bishop."

I gaped at him in complete disbelief. I couldn't even find the words to express how ridiculous it all sounded. Mya and I didn't get along. Never had. There was no way I believed for a second she'd walked into this willingly. "What did you use against her? She hates me."

He scoffed. "Maybe, but she loves her money."

"What does that mean?"

"It means you will marry Mya. End of discussion."

It amazed me how someone could love my mom so much, and still be such a cold, unfeeling bastard. "This outdated, forced marriage bullshit isn't happening."

"Then think of your mother, when you lose every penny she earned to pass down to you. Every minute she spent building this company."

That was a low blow but the son of a bitch didn't care. They were threatening Mya with something. Had to be. Her family had enough money to last a lifetime ten times over.

"Did you think about Mom when you decided to make my life miserable?"

He swallowed hard. "That's enough. I don't want to hear another word about that. That subject's closed."

"My mother's death is closed? Just put a lid on it?"

He ignored my question and turned his back with a dismissive wave of his hand.

"This is happening, Bishop. After you two are married I don't care what you do in your spare time but you won't smear the Shepherd name."

"Did I misunderstand you just now? Did you just tell me to cheat on the down low?" Apparently, there was nothing too revolting for my father.

"You can do whatever you want once your vows are made and our family legacy is safe. I don't care as long as it doesn't become a problem."

Having Shaw as a side piece was the last thing I'd ever do to him. The thought was inconceivable. This conversation was crazy but I could see the determination in my father's eyes. The set of his jaw.

"Now let's put this matter to rest. Our company should be arriving soon and I expect you to represent this family as a good investment."

A sinking feeling settled in my gut. "Who's coming?"

He cocked a brow with confident tilt of his head. "The Vances"

"Are you fucking kidding me?" I was being ambushed by not only my dad but Mya's family? How did I not see this coming?

"Language," he scolded.

I'd never wanted to physically harm my father before but I was furious.

I tried one last time to break through to him. "You wouldn't take this from me. Empty threats really aren't a good look on you, Dad. You want to keep the business in the family. Isn't that why you had me?"

He chose to ignore my question, but that bomb had been dropped when he'd gotten drunk off his ass shortly after my mother died. I was twelve the first time my father admitted he'd never wanted children and that the only reason I existed was because he needed an heir.

"You're mistaken. I'd rather be forgotten altogether than remembered as a laughing stock when my only son runs the business into the ground because he's thinking with the wrong head. So don't think for a moment I wouldn't cut the cord just like that." He snapped his fingers and his lips curled into a sneer. "You're right though. That is exactly what I want. So I'd rather you secure the company's future before you force me into that drastic an action."

"And what if I spend all the money and run it into the ground anyway?"

"Then you'd be pissing all over your mother's memory."

The emotional blow hit hard and sharp, sucking the breath from my lungs just as the doorbell rang.

He smiled. "Our guests have arrived. Don't embarrass this family."

# SEVEN
# BISHOP

WHAT FAMILY? I was an only child with one parent who was anything but fatherly.

With that last warning, he walked away to answer the door with me following behind him. Friendly chatter started the moment he let them in. I recognized the sweet feminine voice of my late mother's best friend. She entered first, wearing a wine-colored form-fitted skirt and some kind of silky shirt. Her husband entered behind her and shook hands with my father and then Mya came through the door last, flawless on the outside as I remembered her.

Her dark hair was smooth and shiny, her dress light blue and hugging her body just enough to hint at her figure but remain classy. She was beautiful but I remained unaffected. She was the first one to lock gazes with me and she sent a timid smile and I refrained from a snort. Timid she was not.

I turned away and strode into the kitchen.

"Bishop, wait up."

Despite my reputation of being a complete asshole, I was raised with manners, so instead of ignoring her, I paused while she caught up. Once she did, she grabbed my hand and pulled me into the long hallway that led to the back deck. Then she tugged me into a slight alcove and smiled.

With a glare, I jerked my arm free. "What the hell are you doing?"

"Rude much?"

"You're the one jerking me all over the place. If you pulled me in here to have your way with me, it's not happening and while I'm on the subject, I'm also not marrying you."

She batted at the air like my words were merely a nuisance. "I barely tolerate you, Bishop. I most definitely am not here to *have my way with you*." Her fingers curled into quotes and she forced a laugh. "The marriage thing... well, that's what we need to discuss."

"Nothing to discuss. It's not happening. Did you agree to this shit?" I crossed my arms and leaned back against the wall.

She placed her hands on her hips and lifted her chin. "Yes, but I didn't have much choice. You want me to give up my inheritance?"

"They are threatening your inheritance?" *Who are these people?*

"My dad is. My mom's in the dark and it's supposed to stay that way. What's yours using against you?"

"My part of the company," I stated flatly.

Her lips parted. "Well, that's all kinds of fucked up."

"It was my mom's company too and he's willing to take it from me. Yeah, I'd say that's fucked up."

After a solemn nod, she pushed her shoulders back. "Well, it won't be a problem because I don't have an issue with it. You keep the company and I keep my inheritance."

"I'm not marrying you. I can't believe you're okay with

it." For someone who didn't talk much, I was finding it hard to keep my voice down. I turned to leave but she latched on to my arm again.

"*Okay* isn't the word I'd use. Resigned is more like it. I've had a few days to sit on it. Why are you so against it? It's not like either of us believe in happily ever after. Unless..." She cocked her head and studied me. "Are you serious about someone?"

"My dad didn't fill you in?" I contemplated how much I was willing to reveal myself and decided *fuck it*. "I'm gay, Mya, and yes I care a lot about someone."

Stone cold expression; she didn't flinch. "Doesn't matter. After we are married, there is no reason we have to share a bed. It's merely a financial transaction. We both keep what belongs to us. We can even split bank accounts."

I gaped. "You can hear yourself, right?"

She placed her hands on her hips and pursed her lips. "Look, I have a boyfriend who knows the score. Deal with yours and then problem solved."

My eyes widened. "You have a boyfriend?"

"Well, I did." She had enough decency to appear slightly disappointed. "I broke up with him before coming tonight."

I shook my head. "You shouldn't have. This isn't happening, Mya."

"Yes, it is," she argued.

"No, it's really not. I'll find a way to get out of this." I was already trying to navigate this horrible situation. It felt as if I'd gotten lost in a nightmare and I wanted to wake up.

"You do that, but I wouldn't hold my breath. I suggest that, until you do, you keep private whatever you have going on, unless you want your father to push you into it sooner."

She lowered her voice. "I don't care either way. But I *won't* lose my inheritance."

"Wait, if I can get out of it, it won't be on you." I realized maybe she'd help me if the blame for any fallout would be placed on me.

"Have you met my father? If my dad loses this merger and I wasn't able to convince you, he'll definitely not be forgiving." Her pretty features twisted in annoyance. "Like I said, I'll do what I need to. But if you can get out of it, that would be great. I wasn't exactly thrilled about breaking up with my boyfriend, but we do what we have to."

"Lucky guy you have there." My undisguised sarcasm earned me a bored look. "I'll handle—"

"There you two are." Mrs. Vance poked her head into the alcove and eyed the two of us like we were a couple kids she expected to find making out. "I'm glad I'm not interrupting but dinner is being served and we don't want to be rude," she addressed her daughter.

"Never." Mya rolled her eyes and we all made our way to the dining room where they'd conveniently placed us together.

I glanced toward my father who was deep in conversation with Mya's dad. He didn't acknowledge we'd joined them. Dinner was tense and I tasted nothing I put in my mouth. Even the smell of perfectly grilled salmon was nauseating.

My knee was squeezed hard beneath the table, and I turned my head to glare at Mya. She leaned toward me. "Act happy. If I can do it, so can you."

"Don't touch me again." I excused myself the minute my plate was cleared, making my way to the back patio.

I'd only been outside a few minutes when the sliding

door opened behind me and I inwardly groaned. "Not now, Mya."

"It's not Mya." Mrs. Vance's voice came from behind me as her heels clacked on the stones. She came to a stop beside me.

My jaw clenched. "I'm sorry. I didn't mean to be disrespectful."

"Is everything all right?" Her tone was laced with worry and I didn't know if I could lie to her and tell her everything was fine. It was far from it. "You didn't look happy at dinner and I'm getting the feeling something is wrong."

Torn, I still hadn't decided how to respond when she let out a long sigh. "Is this your father's and my husband's doing?"

"You didn't know?" I scoffed in disbelief and slid a glance at her.

She crossed her arms and hugged herself. "I suspected. I knew Mya was seeing someone and the engagement seemed rather fast."

"Engagement?" I repeated in confusion.

She appeared bewildered. "Well, yes. The celebratory dinner..." she trailed off with her arm sweeping toward the door.

I stared at her, trying to absorb the information. "Did you say we just had a dinner to celebrate my engagement to Mya?"

She frowned harder and I let out a dark laugh.

"Mrs. Vance, I didn't know that we were celebrating *anything*. I'm being blackmailed into marrying your daughter—no offense—for the sake of merging two companies and the financial gain it will bring my father. Oh, and to cover up the fact that I'm gay and currently with a guy who isn't loaded, which according to my father, is risking the family name and assets. Wonderful man, my father."

She gasped. "What?"

I said nothing and gave her a steady look.

"Does Mya... Is she..."

"Being coerced? Yes. Her inheritance."

Her breath stuttered. "I don't understand."

I shrugged and looked back out into the dark. "Your husband wants to go into business with my father. My dad made him an offer he apparently couldn't refuse."

"I'll speak to him my husband. I just... My daughter isn't a pawn to be traded like a company asset. Your mother and I used to dream of you two marrying, but not like this."

"And you think he'll listen?" I gave her a pointed look.

"No." She whispered as if it hurt her to admit and hugged herself tighter.

"I'm not marrying her," I said firmly. "I'll figure something out."

She sniffled as she retreated toward the door. "I hope so. Marriage is a long time to be miserable."

She spoke as if she knew firsthand what she was talking about. She slid the door shut as she went back inside, leaving me alone again, listening to the night. Crickets chirped and a breeze heavy with humid air wrapped around me, stifling and restricting. The same way I felt when I thought about losing my part of the company. Of disappointing my mom. Of marrying Mya. My throat tightened. Of losing Shaw.

I knew I had to tell him but tell him what? I didn't wait for the Vances to leave and ignored my father's hushed demands that I stop and strode through the door and jumped in my car. As soon as I hit the highway, I dialed Shaw.

"What's up?" The sound of his voice was a balm to my overworked nerves.

"On my way home." I exhaled heavily. "Are you coming over?"

"Sure, but what's wrong?" His tone was cautious.

I hesitated a moment. "What do you mean?"

"You sound off. Something go wrong at your dad's?"

I cleared my throat. I needed to tell him and I would. But first, I needed him to ground me with his calm, easy nature so I could think clearly. There had to be a way out. "The usual. You ready?"

"Uh, yeah. Let me just grab my keys and I'll be on my way." His tone hadn't changed and I knew he'd have questions and I intended to answer them all. It was time to be real with Shaw and tell him everything.

I didn't want to bring him down with me. That was the last thing I'd ever want. Shaw was the light where I was dark. The smile to my frown. He deserved better and I knew it.

"See you soon." I clicked the phone off and sucked in a deep breath. *Okay*, I repeated in my head. Things would be okay.

## EIGHT
## SHAW

BISHOP LAY in the cradle of my legs, spreading them wide with his thick thighs as he moved inside me, thrusting slow and deep. His eyes, dark and intense, never left mine as he took me. The lack of dirty talk was both alarming and making me feel things I promised him I wouldn't. Bathed only by the light of the moon, his expression was hard to make out, but emotion bled through the way he touched me and I touched him back. I wished I could climb inside that brain of his and find out what he was thinking about—how he was feeling. But I was afraid if I asked, I would reveal what was going on in mine. I didn't want this to end. The way he watched my every reaction, I was sure he could see things that I was beginning to understand myself.

He leaned down and pressed a soft, yet firm kiss to my lips, denying me when I parted them and instead kissed the corner of my mouth. His movements slowed further until he was leisurely rocking into me.

"Bishop," I murmured. "What—"

He silenced me with another drugging kiss and shifted

the angle of his hips. I gasped and let the unasked question rest.

"Make me come," I begged when he came up for air.

He paused for a beat before resuming his slow pace. "You'll come."

Whispers too low for me to decipher left his lips and disappeared into the quiet room. He reached between us and gripped my shaft, pumping me to the rhythm he'd set. He was right, the orgasm building was unexpected. Bone deep pleasure swelled to the surface riding the edge of something I hadn't experienced before.

When Bishop's arms began to shake I knew he was close. His shadowed eyes pierced mine and I was helpless not to fall into the deep abyss. The spark ignited into a blazing inferno so immense I wanted to close my eyes and burn for him, but I couldn't—not when he was staring at me so intently, like I was the only thing in the world that mattered. The enormity of what I felt for him surfaced in that one unguarded moment. Though it scared me to my core, I *wanted* him to see me. I wanted him to reciprocate those feelings and the realization was terrifying.

His arms shook harder and my body trembled in response. I let go. My mouth opened in a silent *Oh* as wave after wave of ecstasy wracked my body and I spilled onto my stomach and his hand. The feeling was so powerful I couldn't make a sound. His strokes tapered off as my body spasmed and jerked with aftershocks. And then a deep groan ripped from his throat and he dropped his lips onto mine, kissing me deeper as he thrust through his orgasm. He stilled but continued kissing me like he'd die if he stopped.

"You..." he said against my lips. "I..."

He continued to lie on top of me, unmoving and keeping our lips barely brushing together.

"You, what?" I hesitantly wrapped my hands around his back, rubbing my palms over his slick skin. He didn't stop me so I wrapped my legs around him, holding him in place as his eyes slammed closed.

Seconds, minutes, or maybe hours of silence passed before he untangled himself to clean up. I followed him into the bathroom and took care of myself.

Once we crawled back in bed, I reached out and ran a finger down his thick bicep. "Is everything okay?" A devastating thought crossed my mind. "What was that, Bishop? Was that like..." I swallowed hard as I stared at him. "Was that goodbye?"

He whipped his head to the side and fire in his eyes blazed. "Not even close."

When he didn't elaborate, I still couldn't shake the unease. "And everything's okay?"

He exhaled hard and turned on his side, wrapped an arm around me and dragged me across the sheets until he I was pressed against him. "It's been a long day and I'm tired. I'm...I'm just glad you're here."

I'd known him long enough to know when he was holding back but we were in uncharted territory. I was both relieved and worried. What did this mean for us?

As if he sensed my confusion he threw a leg over mine and anchored me to him.

What he didn't know was that I'd broken the rules. I'd fallen in love with him.

---

BISHOP WAS STILL SLEEPING SOUNDLY when I slipped from bed and dressed. I was starving so I decided to leave him be while I ran down to the kitchen to whip up some breakfast. I beat up some eggs and poured them into a pan, but my mind was on the night before. I broke down each touch, every kiss, analyzing the entire night and planning my next move. I was in a heated debate with myself over whether or not I should tell him how I felt when the doorbell rang.

I frowned, turned off the heat and moved the pan before glancing at the clock. He wasn't expecting anyone that I was aware of.

The knocking began as I made my way to the front door. When I opened the door I smiled at the woman on the other side only to be met with a sour expression. In her designer jeans and top, and purse that probably cost more than my car, she appeared to be well off. When I peeked behind her and saw the shiny sports car, I decided that she was more than well off. She had to be loaded. Like Bishop.

"Can I help you?"

She ripped off her sunglasses and huffed. "Can *you* help *me*?"

I held a firm grip on the door when she tried to step inside. "Whoa. Who are you?"

"Where's Bishop?"

I straightened at his name. "Upstairs. Can I at least tell him who you are before you come barging in?"

She propped her hand on her hips. "He needs to get up and you need to leave. I should have known he'd go running to you. One last time and all."

I blinked several times as I stood unmoving. "Excuse me?"

"You heard me. Play time is over." She leaned as far into the house as she could, pressing up against me. "Bishop!" she screamed and I jerked back. What in the actual fuck was wrong with her?

Thumps sounded from upstairs followed by several more before he appeared at the top of the stairs, wearing a pair of black sweatpants that hung low on his hips. He'd been naked when I'd left the bed, so he must have thrown them on before charging downstairs. His mouth was set in a firm line.

"Tell this asshole to let me in."

I glared at her before focusing on Bishop who slowly descended the stairs. I locked eyes with him. "Who's the chick?"

"Oh, nice," she ground out. "The chick is his fiancée. Get out of my way."

The statement was made with such venom and conviction that my hand fell from the door. My gaze never left Bishop's as I searched for the truth. No way would he keep something like that from me. She took advantage of my lack of response to wiggle by me.

He held my stare, something like uncertainty in his eyes and my throat tightened. Because, no. Bishop was a lot of things, but a liar and cheat weren't among them. He was gay, for fuck's sake. There had to be some kind of explanation. His gaze switched to her as she stood with her hands on her hips, her eyes narrowed to slits, before returning to me

"It's not like that," Bishop began.

"News flash, it's exactly like that." She held up her hand and showed off a miniature iceberg centered in a halo of white gold on her ring finger.

My gaze flew back and forth between the two as confusion, guilt, anger and more confusion coiled in my gut. She was wearing a ring. His ring. My mind attempted to wrap around the idea as my whole body shook.

"Mya, that's enough," Bishop gritted between his teeth.

"Mya," I repeated the unfamiliar name. "Who is she, Bishop? Tell me she's lying. "

It didn't even make sense.

"The daughter of my mom's best friend who has no business being here." He crossed his arms over his bare chest and widened his stance.

"Yeah, well, when you walked out last night, your dad wasn't very happy. And guess what? You didn't answer your phone this morning so he decided he was coming to talk to you here and asked that I join him. You're lucky I got here first. You need to get rid of him." Her gaze cut to me.

"Hold on," I interrupted what appeared to be the beginning of a monumental fight. I only needed a few answers and if he didn't call her an outright liar, then they could blow the whole place up for all I cared. Looking at Bishop made me physically ill but I swallowed hard and held his gaze. "You're engaged? To her? You were with her at your dad's last night?"

"Are you fucking hard of hearing?" She smirked as she looked me over. "When your dad explained what was going on this morning and what I should expect, he was right about one thing."

"Don't," Bishop warned.

I glanced down, following her haughty stare, and my cheeks flushed. I tugged on the hem of my sophomore year, worn Saints t-shirt that I'd thrown on over my old athletic shorts before I came downstairs. I was dressed comfortably but with the way she peered down her nose at me, you'd think I was covered in dirt. I'd never felt uncomfortable around Bishop, and the difference in how much money we had in our bank accounts had never bothered me. But now..."What was your dad right about?"

"You don't belong with him and we both know it," Mya

said and I winced as the truth slammed into my chest. "To each their own, but now you've become my problem."

"Dammit, Mya, that's enough." Bishop squeezed between us.

I backed up and peered around him, meeting her glare again. "Did you know about me?"

"Knew that he was fucking around with a plaything? Of course I did!" She laughed. "Although, I was surprised not to see the blue piece of junk car in the driveway like I expected. Must be in the garage."

"Mya!" Bishop roared in a way I'd never heard. His voice echoed off the walls with so much menace it sent chills crawling over my skin.

He was seething, but still hadn't denied it. My stomach bottomed out. I didn't give two shits what she thought about my clothes or my car. But I did care that those things prevented the chance of anyone ever taking Bishop and me seriously, which made me feel like I wasn't good enough. Not that I'd even talked to him about that yet. Small mercies.

I backed toward the stairs. "I think I'm going to head out. This is just..." *What the fuck was it?*

"Shaw—" He moved toward me before shiny pink nails sank into his arm.

"We need to talk about this," she hissed.

"It can wait." He ripped his arm from her grip and followed me upstairs.

The room smelled of him. And me. My throat tightened as I gathered my clothes that were strewn around the room from the night before.

"I had no idea she was going to show up this morning," Bishop said as he leaned against the doorframe. "Are you going to let me explain?"

I glanced over my shoulder as I tucked my cheap wallet into my pocket. Suddenly everything I owned felt out of place in his home. "I'm not sure it would matter."

"Don't do that," he growled.

I snatched my keys from the dresser then stepped into his space as I readied to leave. "Is she or is she not your fiancée?"

He didn't answer immediately and my heart sank further.

"No. It's complicated." He rubbed his eyes. "But I'm not marrying her."

"Does she know that? I'm getting the impression that she doesn't."

He hesitated again and I shoved by to get out of the room that, only an hour before, I'd woken up in with him wrapped around me.

"I've told her," he said as he followed me.

"She has a ring on her finger that says otherwise."

"She must have bought that herself. You have no idea what I'm up against."

I paused before descending the stairs and lowered my voice. "I *wouldn't* know. You're right. Why didn't you tell me before you fucked me last night? I think I deserved to know or understand before running into a damn surprise attack this morning. You might as well have lied to me."

His jaw clenched. "It's a recent development and I don't plan on following through with it. But I *did* plan on talking to you about it today, I swear."

"You couldn't like explain it to me before you stuck your cock in me? What if I wasn't okay with it? *News flash*, isn't that what she said? I'm not okay with it."

"I planned on telling you," he repeated with urgency.

"When? After the marriage?"

"No, today, and stop saying marriage." His expression screwed up with distaste.

"So you planned to tell me today that you recently got engaged to someone I've never heard you speak a word about." I shook my head in disbelief.

"I've never *had* a reason to talk about her because I haven't even seen Mya in forever."

"That doesn't make any of this okay." The hurt and humiliation drilled deeper and deeper and I couldn't see a way to make it right. Not only had he withheld something I felt was important to know, but I could see that my growing feelings for him only meant disaster for me. If for some reason he returned them, she was right, I didn't fit in his world. Never would.

"Come on, Shaw. This happened last night and I'm not marrying her." We both paused, not moving and staring at each other. He sighed and ran his hand through his thick hair. "I don't know what to do with this mess."

I felt the slap in the face as real as if he'd actually put his hands on me.

"I'm the mess."

"Yes." He cursed. "Not like that. The situation is a clusterfuck of my dad's making."

"How does this even happen? Does she know you're gay? Why the fuck are you semi-engaged to a woman?" The questions spilled from my mouth as my head spun with the weird situation we'd landed in.

"Yes, she knows. My dad knows, too, and set the whole insane thing up."

"I don't understand any of it." My shoulders were rigid as he reached for me. When I jerked away, he ran his hands through his outgrown wavy hair again and then shoved them into his pocket. "You still should have told me. That's fucked up. You know, they are right though. What are you doing with someone like me anyway?"

"Don't *ever* talk about yourself like that, damn it. I—"

"If you two are done and you're ready to listen, your dad is on his way!" Mya's voice reminded me that she waited downstairs and probably heard part of our conversation, which did embarrass me.

"What the fucking shit? Did you call him?" Bishop yelled.

She came into view at the bottom of the steps and rolled her eyes. "I told you he asked me to join him and even mentioned I got here first."

I needed to get away from this bullshit. "I'm leaving. I'll get the rest of my stuff later."

I thumped down the stairs and she stepped in front of me.

"You two are over. Understand?" she gritted through her teeth.

"Like hell," Bishop said as I stated the opposite, "Correct."

"What the fuck, Shaw?" he boomed.

"I'm not getting into this...whatever this is. You have a fucking fiancée and I clearly don't belong in the middle of this situation."

"Right, because it was just fun anyway." He sneered and my stomach clenched.

"You said it." I swallowed hard to cover the hitch in my voice.

The sound of an engine pulling into the driveway cut off any retort he may have had and got my feet moving. Things were bad enough. I didn't want to deal with his dad. Bishop cursed loud behind me. When I escaped through the door to the garage no one stopped me. I hit the button and the door began rolling up. I jumped in my car.

As I sat in my small sedan with its not-good-enough blue chipped paint, I glanced in my mirror at the new arrival. The luxury car was parked behind Bishop's and belonged to Mr. Shepherd. He climbed out and slipped his sunglasses from his face, folded them and tossed them back into the driver's seat. Though I'd never met him and he never attended our games, I'd have identified him on spot. He and Bishop were nearly identical, albeit decades apart.

He closed the car door then his attention shifted to me. His face was stone, no expression at all, as he lost interest in me and headed for the front door. My heart shattered as if it had been hit with an expensive sledgehammer. The clarity of my true feelings for Bishop, which I'd only realized a few hours ago, had been warped by the ugly reality.

I was never going to fit in his world in a permanent sense and entertaining the idea was ridiculous. We were a deal. No promises. Sex between friends, convenient and hot, that would end one day with no hard feelings. Well there were feelings and they weren't pleasant. And I was *in fucking love* with him. How did that happen? I beat my hand on the steering wheel.

I made myself start the car and drove back to my small dorm, where I sat on my bed and stared down at my shoes. Everything became clearer as the minutes passed. Even my damned shoes suddenly seemed shabby. Trying to process what had just gone down, I went over our conversations. He said they weren't engaged, or maybe he didn't. She said they were. But what reason did he have to lie? I didn't know her. But he was with her the night before. Had he taken her to dinner with his dad? The thought made me nauseated.

I didn't want to be locked in a room with my thoughts

and nothing to ease them and I definitely wasn't calling Bishop. He'd let her blindside me no matter what the hell was going on. Without hesitation, I picked up my phone to text Nash. I couldn't tell him why, but it wouldn't be unusual for me to call at any hour asking him to work out, though Bishop usually went with us.

*Bishop.*

He had a fiancée. There was more to it, but he shouldn't have slept with me again until he had that sorted. Or at least until he told me. But more than anything, the haze that had prevented me from seeing how different we truly were had been lifted. At our core we were a perfect match, at least I thought so. But circumstances had left us worlds apart.

"What the fuck," I said out loud this time. My fingers hovered over the keyboard screen. My hands were shaking too bad to text so I hit call.

"Hello?" His rich voice was thick with sleep.

"Get your ass out of bed. I need a workout partner." And a distraction.

"Why? What time is it?" There was a moment of silence. "Dude, we don't have to be there for another two hours. And where's your other half?" He yawned.

"He's busy." True, yet vague. It'd have to do because I had no idea what to say.

"Everything all right?" He sounded more alert and the creak of a mattress came across the line.

"Who's that?" a familiar half-asleep voice said in the background. "Tell them to go away."

"Give me twenty and I'll meet you there." The phone went silent and I glanced at the screen.

He'd hung up on me, and that had been my Rendon's voice. My little brother. *You've got to be fucking kidding me.*

I curled forward and hung my head. This day was

getting worse by the minute. I had already been worried when Nash met my brother at the NFL draft viewing party for Rush a few months ago. Now it seemed like I'd had reason to be. Between Bishop, Mya, Mr. Shepherd, Nash and Rendon I wasn't sure I was going to make it through the day without losing my mind.

I missed Rush and Torin. One had recently been drafted by the Texas Warriors and the other graduated, leaving me with two less people to call up. Maybe they'd know what to do. I laughed aloud, though nothing was funny, because Bishop wasn't easy to figure out on the best day.

# NINE
## BISHOP

"I THOUGHT I'd made myself clear about that boy." My dad paced back and forth in my living room. "You were to stop seeing him and start courting Mya."

Mya had taken an uninvited seat on my couch and I leaned against the wall furthest from them. There was no reasoning with Patrick Shepherd.

"I'm sorry. Did you just say courting?" For someone who was continuously building a business, creating the most *It* clubs in the country, you'd think that his vocabulary would have kept up to date as well. "Never once in all that bullshit you spouted, did you say I had to start dating her."

"For such a smart kid..." He walked over to the portrait of my mother and paused. "When you marry someone you should start by courting them first."

"Maybe if it's not arranged. In this case it seems pointless, don't you think?"

He turned around with a blank expression. "I suppose you are correct. But what of the distress you would cause her if you were caught with him?"

I scrubbed my hands over my face. "I haven't agreed to

anything. In fact I believe I strongly voiced my position against it."

If I ever married, I would at least like to tolerate my significant other's fucking company. After the shit she pulled earlier with Shaw, I hated her. My relationship with him was as good as finished, but as soon as I could get rid of these two monsters, I was going to track him down.

"You're willing to give up hundreds of millions?" Mya interrupted my thoughts. Her arms were crossed as she leaned back into the cushions. "Because I'm not."

I hesitated. The problem wasn't black and white as she suggested. The ultimatum had been sprung on me less than twenty-four hours ago. My past, present and future revised by a single decision made by my father, who didn't care about me or my happiness. It was going to take more than a few hours to process. The thought of having to spend the rest of my life crammed between these two was depressing as hell. I wished they would go away so I could think.

Her smile grew victorious and she pounced on that sliver of doubt. "I didn't think so, especially over a booty call."

Lighting fast, I was off the wall, standing rigid with a finger pointed at her. "He's more than that. Shaw is my friend—my only *real* friend—so don't cheapen that shit. He's been the only good thing to happen to me in a really long time and you insulted him repeatedly this morning. Trust me, your life would be miserable with me. I'd make sure of it."

She rolled her eyes.

"The girl has a point. You should listen to her," my dad said, as if I hadn't spoken a word.

I checked out of the conversation. It wasn't going anywhere.

As they continued to lecture me on what I should be doing and the mistakes I was making, my gaze drifted to the large wall clock. I watched as the minutes ticked by and kept track of how much time had passed since Shaw had taken off. I needed to catch up to him and make him understand. The situation was complicated and the stakes were huge.

The only way to close the door on this marriage talk would be to let go of the only future I'd ever prepared for. My dad wasn't going to budge.

My attention was drawn to my mom's portrait again. She and my grandmother were the only family I'd ever known. The only ones that had ever loved me, and I lost them both on the same day. My mother had been blind to the way my dad had loved her but not me. But she'd always been enough. The business was my only connection to her. Could I really step away from that?

"Bishop." My name snapped off my father's tongue. "Feel free to contribute to the conversation."

I cocked my head to the side. "Does it matter what I have to say?"

My father's eyes narrowed. "A quick agreement and a promise to stop seeing that boy would save me a lot of time."

"Well I hate to break it to you, Dad. You can't always get what you want."

His coloring deepened and his lips thinned. He wasn't used to anyone fighting back. Everyone kissed his ass, and before all of this marriage talk, I had no reason to get in his way.

"Careful. You may say something you'll regret." He stiffened his back and squared his shoulders.

"Doubtful." I crossed the room, pausing at the base of the stairs. I had somewhere I needed to be.

"So you've made a decision then?" he bit out.

"Sure, I've decided I really need to be going, so if you two could see yourselves out..." I swept my arm in the direction of the door. "Now would be appreciated."

"Ungrateful. Unreasonable," he muttered. "Why must you be so difficult?"

"One, I don't love her. Two, I'm fucking gay. And three, the whole thing is stupid and insane. You aren't listening and I'm honestly not sure what to say anymore." When he went to open his mouth again, I sighed and began climbing the stairs. "I'm leaving, so you both need to get out of my house."

I paused halfway up and glanced back, not surprised at all to see they hadn't budged. Seeing the resolve in my face, Mya stood with a huff and marched to the door without a word. I could at least sympathize with her frustration. My father strolled closer, pausing by the first step as I looked down on him. "Don't forget who you are talking to, Bishop."

I ground my molars together. "Your point?"

"I am really losing my patience." He let that sink in before sauntering off and closing the front door behind him.

Once I heard his car pulling away, I ran the rest of the way to the second floor, grabbed my keys and gear bag, since I wouldn't have time to come back before I had to report for conditioning, and hurried out to my car. I called Shaw and as expected, he didn't answer, so I cranked the engine and headed toward the school.

When I arrived on campus the first thing I did was stop by Shaw's dorm. No sound came from inside and he didn't answer when I knocked. The only other place he'd have gone was to the athletic center so I hopped back into my car and circled the school. I spotted both Shaw's and Nash's cars in the parking lot and pulled into the space between them.

I grabbed my bag and made my way inside, crossed the open field and entered the weight room. The place was empty except for two people. My gaze instantly focused on the blond doing arm curls next to Nash. His eyes were fixated on the weight in his hand.

"Yo, Bishop." My gaze slid over to Nash. "You'd better take that creepy ass look on your face somewhere else. Like the locker-room and then come partner with Shaw. He isn't listening to me."

That grabbed my attention and my attention flew back to Shaw. He was straining as he pumped his arm fast. I stepped forward and saw how red his face was. Sweat dotted his brow and his veins were swollen. The cords of his neck pulled taut as he grimaced. I checked on how much he was using. Way too much.

"He's going to end up injured or something stupid. What the hell has gotten into him?" Nash set down his own weights

"Stop talking like I'm not right here," Shaw snarled and set down the dumbbell. He glanced at me for the first time since I arrived and glared. "What do you want?"

Beneath the anger was hurt, it was etched in his eyes and the repeated bobbing of his Adam's apple, and it was my fault.

"Oookay." Nash's gaze flicked between the two of us. "Something's going on between you two. You both banging the same chick or something? Do y'all even bang chicks? Or like bang at all? You know, I never see either of you with anyone. Maybe that's the problem. You both need some pussy."

"Shut the fuck up, Nash." I lashed out and immediately

felt bad, but I never wanted to picture Shaw with someone else. I wouldn't know how I'd handle it.

Nash scowled and stood before reaching for his water. "Well, that was rude. Seriously, what's up?"

"No, maybe he has a point." Shaw gave me a defiant stare. "It's been a while. Maybe that is what I need."

My heart hammered, but instead of rising to the bait, I spun around and headed for the locker-room. In minutes, I was dressed out, back in the weight room and prowling toward Shaw, bypassing Nash who'd moved on to the stationary bike. He was barely moving his legs and Shaw was still on the bench, staring at the ground.

"Hell no," he said when I grabbed the bench next to him.

I raised a brow. "Yes—your favorite word. If I remember correctly, you said it several times last night."

Nash butted in again. "You guys are acting weirder than usual and I'm not dense. That sounded extremely sexual. Maybe it's not the right time to bring this up, but that was a total joke about the chick by the way. Everyone knows you two are banging each other."

Shaw locked eyes with me. His jaw dropped. My eyes widened.

"Don't look so surprised. Rush and Torin didn't hide it any better than you two. No one wants to say anything since you're possibly psychotic and have enough money and resources to ruin any one of our lives."

That grabbed my attention and I scowled. No one thought I was that bad.

He caught my eye. "True story."

"Damn it, Nash," Shaw snapped. "I'm sick and tired of y'all thinking he's some kind of bad guy."

"I don't." He shrugged. "I think he's an asshole, and as of two minutes ago, I'm pretty sure you did too."

"He *is* an asshole," Shaw stated and looked back at me.

I was still surprised everyone knew and neither of us was defending ourselves. *I don't give a fuck anymore.*

"I'm gay." There, I said it out loud. No taking it back and when I met Shaw's eyes again, I hoped he knew I'd done it for him. However this thing turned out, he mattered a hell of a lot more than what people thought of me. The only real reason I'd kept it to myself was a non-issue since my dad was now aware. I had nothing to lose, except Shaw. And it killed me that I still might.

Nash didn't appear fazed. "Yeah, I got that when I said we all know you are doing the deed. Is this your official coming out party?"

No, this was me proving a point to Shaw.

Shaw's face whipped to the side where Nash stood. "You're fucking my little brother!"

Nash's eyes widened and he stopped pedaling. "What the fuck, Shaw? Why would you think—"

"Cut the crap. I heard him on the phone."

"I don't know what you think you heard." He shook his head quickly. "But you're mistaken."

"Really? Maybe I should call him and see what he has to say." Shaw tilted his head. "What are you doing with him, Nash? He's my little brother. Not some fuck and ditch you're used to."

Nash held up his hands. "Fine, I'll stay out of your business."

"Yeah, you have your own shit and I should kick your ass for going near him."

Wisely, Nash didn't respond to the comment and

picked up the pace. His legs moved quicker and he studied the timer.

"We need to talk," I whispered to Shaw.

"Oh? Did you and your dad get everything settled?"

How did I handle this question? No, nothing was settled, but I knew what I wanted. He looked back at me with eyes that pleaded with me to fix this. *Why can't I pull the damn plug?*

I paused too long and he stood up. "Don't worry about it. We both know nothing between us would have lasted anyway."

He stormed off.

"Fuck!" I was madder at myself than anyone because now I'd really messed up. I'd given him hope and squashed it with my damn issues and inability to fucking make up my damn fucking mind. "Shit!"

Nash whistled. "Not tryin' to pry but you may want to give him time to cool off. You too."

"Mind your own business, Nash." I picked up the weights Shaw had set down and started my own frustration infused reps.

He held up his hands. "Just an idea."

"Well, you have your own issues to deal with."

"Truth," he muttered.

## TEN
# SHAW

MY ALARM CLOCK woke me up thirty minutes before time to get ready for conditioning, and I lay in bed like I didn't need to get my ass moving. I toyed with my phone, turning it in circles. I'd read the texts from Bishop over the last two days so many times that I'd memorized them word for word.

*"I want to explain everything."*

*"You're not going to respond?"*

*"I know you hate me right now. Just hear me out."*

*"I know you're home and ignoring me when I knock. Just give me a few minutes and then you can decide what you want to do."*

*"Fine. The night of the dinner, my dad threatened to take away my part of the company if I didn't call it off with you. He said I had to marry Mya. I had no idea she and her family would be there. Neither of us wanted this. You have to know that."*

*"I should have told you that night. I didn't plan on going through with it but also needed you. It was a selfish move."*

*"I'm sorry."*

*"Answer me, Wakefield. We really need to talk and I'd rather not do it by text."*

When he sent the first message, I'd managed to hold off all of five minutes before I caved and read it. They'd started from the time we left conditioning on the morning of the blowup. For two entire days I'd managed to avoid him. I kept to crowds so he couldn't catch me alone and resisted the temptation to answer the door when he'd stopped by. His messages went unanswered, and I didn't even know if I was doing the right thing. It hurt.

Was I mad? Hell yes. But I'd also known there was a reason and probably would have come to the conclusion on my own if I hadn't been blindsided and felt so betrayed. He wasn't interested in her. I knew that. He wasn't going to turn straight, cheat on me and get engaged all in one night.

*Cheat on me.* I scoffed at the thought, but that's exactly what it felt like.

I realized I'd fallen in love with him and then *bam,* he's engaged. I wanted to talk to him and hear him out. But even knowing what was going on, I was afraid he was going to have to go through with it to keep his spot in the company. And in the unlikely event he got out of the non-engagement and stayed with the company, his dad would always cause tension and make our lives hell. Bishop would suffer the most.

The worst thing that could happen is if he were to cut ties with his dad and the business. Even if he was willing to do it, I'd never let him. He wanted it too bad and had already put in three years of school working toward it. And how was I supposed to measure up to losing that kind of fortune? I couldn't.

Our relationship was over. My stomach heaved. If I'd

eaten much of anything over the last two days I wouldn't have been able to keep it down.

I glanced at the clock and realized I was already late.

"Shit," I muttered and rolled out of bed on unsteady legs and made my way to the tiny bathroom. I caught sight of my reflection in the mirror and winced. A few days worth of stubble had gone unattended and dark circles from lack of sleep under my eyes made me appear half-dead. My short hair was a mess of tangles and odd tufts sticking up with gnarly bed head from tossing and turning. I averted my eyes from my pathetic image. I felt just as lousy on the inside.

Getting ready zapped my energy, but I pushed myself once I left the dorm and ran the entire way to the athletic center. The more I ran the more the burn distracted me.

"Cutting it close," our conditioning coach said as he looked me over with a frown. "You feelin' all right, Wakefield?"

"Yeah, I'm good." I lied.

"Okay then. Go dress out." He sounded skeptical.

I changed into my workout clothes and met the rest of the team back on the field. *He* was already there. His gaze focused on me, burning like hot coals against my skin. I resisted the urge to seek him out. Once, it had been so natural and it was a struggle to stop myself. The feeling lingered as I listened to coach explain how he planned to torture us.

"Today we are going to take the hill. You'll sprint up and back five times." His attention bounced to each one of us.

I groaned under my breath. The hill was a steep incline that tested your calves and thighs on the first pass. Five times and we'd wish we were dead. It appeared I was facing a very rough morning.

Coach clapped. “Let’s move out!”

Five minutes later we stood at the base of the hill affectionately named by the locals “The Sugar Land Mountain”.

We lined up in rows. I took the first and I wasn’t surprised at all when Bishop lined up next to me. He didn’t say a word and he didn’t need to.

Coach blew the whistle and I took off, Bishop matching me stride-for-stride. When I sped up, so did he. When I became winded and slowed, he jogged beside me. We’d run the drill so many times and I hated them. His silent support reminded me how in sync we were. I hated him for it. Except that I didn’t.

By the time we reached our starting point from the fifth round trip, I dropped my hands on my knees and struggled for breath. When that proved difficult, I stood and placed my hands on my hips and slowly walked it off.

“Here.” Bishop stepped in front of me with a half-empty bottle of water.

I took it and chugged the other half.

“Thanks,” I mumbled and handed him back the empty bottle.

He glanced at it with a small quirk of his lips that quickly disappeared. “Shaw, can—”

The whistle blew. “Time to head back. Good job, boys.”

“Figures, the one time you allow me in your space,” Bishop grumbled and my traitorous heart agreed.

The lot of us dragged ass on our way back to the center and hauled our weary bodies into the showers. Bishop’s attention never wavered from me and he didn’t seem to care about witnesses. Yet, he said nothing and exited the locker-room ahead of me.

Once dressed, I slung my bag over my shoulder and headed for the entrance. I wasn’t the slightest bit surprised to find him waiting at the door. After I passed by, Bishop took up next to me without saying a word. The fact that I had put myself in that position wasn't lost on me. We did need to talk. The whole situation ate at me and would continue to, especially if he kept reminding me how happy he made me when we were together.

I set off on foot, following the paved walkways toward my dorm.

"Tell me this is driving you crazy too," he finally said. "I'm not alone in this. I know it. Please just talk to me."

"Why? You didn't." I was ready to talk, but I was still mad about with how he'd handled things. He should have been honest in the first place.

But I was in love with the brute.

"Well if you'd let me explain, I'll tell you everything." He sighed. "Did you read my texts?"

I refused to look at him. "Yeah, I did."

He cleared his throat. "I really am sorry for everything."

I closed my eyes and then glanced over at him. "I know. So am I."

When he shot me an inquisitive expression, I explained. "I shouldn't have avoided you. I just don't know how to handle any of this. It's confusing and it sucks."

"That's putting it lightly. Can we go somewhere to talk?" He adjusted the strap on his bag as we took a shortcut over a large grassy area toward my dorm.

"Maybe. One question first. Are you still 'engaged'?" I curled my fingers into quotes.

"I'm not engaged," Bishop muttered. "Not really."

"You either are or aren't. This back and forth can't last forever. It's messing with my head."

"I know and I want to talk to you about it," he insisted. "I never wanted to string you along or hurt you. I'm just...

I'm just messed up and don't know what I'm doing. This doesn't feel right."

"Because it's not." My voice cracked under the pressure of keeping my composure, which was hard to do with him so close I could smell his body wash. "Your dad thinks I'm trash and he wants me gone bad enough to shackle you with a ball and chain."

Bishop growled. "We both know that's a load of shit."

I dug my toes into the grass and spun toward him. "Is it? He's forcing you to marry some chick you don't even like to get rid of me."

"Well..." He faltered. "Please don't listen to that asshole, Shaw. You're more than good enough and probably better than I deserve."

"That's not true at all." How could he even think that?

"Anyway," he continued, "he doesn't approve of me being gay though he hasn't said it outright. That's the real reason whether he admits it or not."

My shoulders stiffened and my lip curled in disgust. "Your dad..."

"Trust me, I know." He rubbed his eyes. "He knew about us. All along."

"What do you mean?" My brow furrowed.

"He told me there wasn't much he didn't know when he made it his business to know. He also said he hadn't stepped in before now because he didn't think I'd go public about being gay."

"When did you go public?" I was getting more confused.

"This was part of what I wanted to tell you. I had so much to explain that morning when they showed up. I messed up so bad, I know."

"Well, I'm here so tell me."

"Uh, the club..."

My eyes widened. "Did someone see us?"

"Sort of. There was a security camera and no one usually has a reason to monitor that hall. But I didn't know about it or that my dad received notifications when the security code is used to open the door." He reached a hand toward me and then pulled it back. "I'm sorry, Shaw."

"You mean there's a video of us?" I was too emotionally drained to even register shock. In the grand scheme of everything going on, I'd lost my ability to be surprised.

"My dad would have erased that evidence the moment he became aware of it." He blew out a breath. "There's more. So when he saw that, he went digging for info on you."

"Why would he do that if he already knew about me?"

"My guess is he was prepping for war. He wanted all the ammo on you as possible. Not that any of it has a damn thing to do with his real issue."

"Well, what did he say?"

"Uh, he used the excuse that you already know about." Bishop's jaw clenched.

"That I'm basically poor trash who doesn't belong with you," I summed up everything I'd heard from Mya and now this.

"I don't want to talk about that anymore. Shaw, we both know that's not true so let that go. Please."

"I'm not ashamed of who I am, Bishop," I assured him.

"Good. Well, I said I'd tell you everything and I meant it." He tilted his head. "Will you let me tell you everything?"

"There's more?"

"Shaw, I want to tell you about my mom."

I stilled. "You do?"

He nodded and I stared back at him. "You don't have to."

"Please let me." With the vulnerable way he'd asked, there was no way I'd refuse.

I nodded slowly. "Yeah, okay. Of course."

Bishop stuffed his hands in his shorts pockets and glanced around. "You want to do this here?"

Looking around, I decided that although campus was dead, it wasn't an appropriate place for something like that. "Follow me."

# ELEVEN
# SHAW

I LED him a quarter mile to a public park adjacent to my dorm and snagged a bench in the deserted picnic area. We dropped our gear bags and Bishop sat next to me, albeit leaving two feet of space between us that felt like a black void.

"Where do I begin?" He rubbed his hands on his shorts.

"Wherever you feel comfortable."

He nodded. "Okay, my mom... I know I haven't told you about her. There were many times I almost did, but to try to keep some distance"—he winced—"I kept it to myself."

"I understand." And I did. It wasn't part of our deal and he wasn't obligated to share his life with me. There had always been a reason we didn't dig too deep. And I'd gone and fallen in love with him anyway.

"My mom." He cleared his throat and swept his hair from his forehead. "Uh, my mom died when I was twelve, which I told you. It was a car wreck and my dad was driving."

He clenched his teeth and balled his fists. Automatically, my hands moved to his and squeezed. "You don't have to—"

"I want to." He relaxed his hands. "It was their fifteenth anniversary, so they'd gone up to Denver for a getaway and left me with my grandmother. On the third morning, when I went down for breakfast, my grandmother was sitting at the kitchen table with a blank expression." He exhaled hard and shook his head. "I'll never forget the way she just shut down. I'd never seen her like that. When she finally noticed me standing there, she told me to sit. So I did. And she told me what had happened."

He paused, taking slow, rhythmic breaths as he gathered himself.

"They'd gone out to dinner and on the way back to their hotel, my dad hit a patch of ice. The car spun and hit a telephone pole. My mother's side caved in and she died on impact." He sniffed and I realized he was holding back tears. Bishop Shepherd was breaking in front of me. I squeezed his hands tighter and he shot me a small smile. "Well, that was the full story until my dad got raving drunk the week after the funeral."

I scooted closer and he seemed to relax more.

"The bastard was driving too fast. He'd taken a business call while on their fucking night out. Romantic, huh?" He pursed his lips. "A contractor backed out of a job and it was going to delay a club's opening, so he threw money on the table and dragged my mom out of the restaurant. He was pissed and said he snapped at her and was driving recklessly in his hurry to get back. He did hit ice, but because he tried to go through a red light and they almost got hit.

"He said my mom asked him to pull over—that she'd drive. I just imagined her over and over, begging him to stop while he was telling me this. He kept saying it was his fault and then he blamed the contractor. It went in circles until he passed out in the middle of his office floor. I was twelve years old and horrified."

He looked at me, midnight eyes full of sorrow. "He killed my mom, Shaw. Intentional or not. If he'd just calmed down before he got behind the wheel..."

"You've never told him what he said?" I resolved to never give him shit about the way he drove ever again.

He gave a humorless chuckle. "Of course I did. He said I'd had a nightmare and imagined it. The next day he got on a plane and was gone for two weeks on a *business trip*. He hired a nanny to keep an eye on me." He said the words with a sneer. "I was just a kid and had lost my mom, my dad didn't want me, and my grandmother couldn't handle any of it.

"And I still have no clue where he went but he looked like shit and lost a lot of weight while he was away. The thing is, I know he loved my mom. Like the real deal. But she still came after business and him thinking he's king of every damn thing."

"What about your grandma? Did she know what really happened?" I asked.

He hung his head. "My grandma was a wreck and I was too young. I couldn't tell her he was the reason she'd died, that it wasn't just a stroke of bad luck. I didn't have many friends back then, and the ones I did have backed off when I sort of checked out. I had a hard time coming to terms with losing her. Maybe it was the lack of having someone to confide in, but I stopped trusting anyone after that, I guess."

"Do you think you'll ever forgive him?" I wouldn't blame him if he didn't.

"No. There may have been a time when I'd have tried to understand, but nothing changed. If anything he got worse and he buried himself in work." He sniffed again. "You know he didn't even want kids? But he did want an heir. You can imagine how happy he was when I turned out to be a boy so the Shepherd name would live on." He frowned. "Problem fixed. He let that little detail slip that night too."

"Bishop, I'm so sorry about your mom. I'm sorry about all of it. I had no idea." He turned his hands over and wove our fingers together.

"I know. But I told you that stuff to explain myself—why the company means so much to me. My mom... She used to take me to the office. We'd act like I was older and work side-by-side." He smiled to himself. "She always said how amazing it was going to be when I actually *was* older."

"That sounds really nice," I agreed, and his grin turned somber.

"Yeah, but that's just a dream now. I guess I felt like I needed to see it through. Live the dream for her. It's what I've worked for and the only thing I'd ever planned on doing with my life." He stared down at our hands. "I don't know anymore."

We sat in silence until he broke it. "My dad suggested I keep you as a side piece."

This shift in topics was abrupt and my gaze jerked to his. "Seriously?"

"Don't act so shocked. He's something else." He shook his head. "What do we do?"

I blew out a breath. "Seems there aren't a lot of options."

"This can't be the end," Bishop whispered.

"I don't see a way around it." My nerves were shot. This whole experience was emotionally taxing and it didn't appear to have a bright side.

Bishop grip tightened. "What if I just..."

"Just what?"

Bishop released my hands and I pulled them back. He leaned forward, elbows on his knees.

"I can't believe this shit," he whispered. "I honestly thought maybe, just one place in his cold heart might have an ounce of morality and he would let this go. Or I just hoped."

I turned my head away to hide my disappointment and stared off into the tree line. Birds chirped and a squirrel ran up the tree. My life was falling apart and everything else kept moving along.

"This isn't fair to either of us." I glanced back at him.

"So what do we do?" His eyes were full of uncertainty as he asked me for a solution, but I had none.

"I don't know. I can't answer that for you. Your dad has tied your hands." I hunched over next to him and picked at the grass by my shoes.

More minutes of silence passed. There was one thing I needed to know or it would bother me the rest of my life. "I've had something on my mind for days now and since we are being honest, I need it off my chest."

His brow furrowed. "Okay, what is it?"

"The night you came home from your dad's and I came over"—my cheeks heated—"things were different, right?"

Bishop gave me a small smile. "Yeah, they were."

"What was that?"

He stared at me, unmoving, and his mouth opened then closed before he sighed. "I think it would only make things worse for both of us."

He was right. Maybe it was better left alone. "Yeah, probably."

"This is such bullshit." Bishop stood and paced in front of the bench and I hung my head. "What if..."

"You said that already." I squeezed my eyes shut. It was

time to face the truth. I stood as well. "I think I should head home."

Bishop paused his pacing. "To the dorm."

"Where else would I go?" I held my hands out at my sides.

"I don't want you to go anywhere. I don't want to do this without you." His expression had shifted and he looked panicked.

I frowned and took a step toward him, out of habit, but made myself stop. "Do what?"

"Everything. All of it." He took a step toward me. "Fucking life, I don't want to do any of it without you."

"Don't..." I blinked and took a stuttering breath. "Don't say that kind of stuff to me when you know it's not possible."

I hadn't noticed before but Bishop's arms were shaking and he swallowed so hard I heard it. "It doesn't make it any less true."

"You won't have to do it alone." My stomach heaved and I turned away while I took a moment to regain my composure before turning back. "When I said we'd walk away as friends, I meant it. I need time but I'll be there for you. I promise."

No matter how much it killed me. He'd been through enough and I'd rather be his friend than nothing at all. Eventually.

"As friends." His tone was hollow and resigned.

I shrugged. "What else could we be?"

"Fuck!" Bishop yelled. A couple who had just entered the park turned around and scurried off.

I couldn't stand there and hear anymore. My fucking heart was bleeding and the longer I stayed, the worse it got. I lifted my bag onto my shoulder.

"Please." The choked word coming from Bishop caused my heart to stall and I squeezed my eyes closed.

I paused. I debated. I loved him.

"I'm not going to be the reason you lose everything you dreamed of with your mom, Bishop. I can't even compete with that." He stayed silent so I powered on. "This is something you want and your dad has put a price on it. And that includes me walking away to give you what you want." I swallowed hard. "Even if it tears me apart, I'll be the one to do it so you don't have to. And once everything settles down, then..."

After everything he'd told me, I wouldn't—*couldn't*—get in the way of that. So I turned around and walked away, after he had spilled his damn heart to me. My stomach twisted and my chest rattled with shaky breaths. It made me physically ill and every step away felt like a mistake. But the alternative was to leave us in this limbo where he felt he had to choose between me and his mom. The living and the dead.

He hadn't said he loved me and I couldn't fault him for that. You couldn't make someone love you back. But he cared. A lot. I hadn't told him how I felt and I was glad. He didn't need that on his shoulders as well. He was already carrying enough baggage.

When I got back to my dorm, I shut the door behind me and slid down one of the many barriers between me and Bishop, landing on my ass and thumped my head back against the wood. Had I done the right thing?

I lost track of how long I sat there, stewing in my thoughts, when the door shook against my back with three rapid knocks. I climbed to my feet and closed my eyes. I knew it was Bishop. I debated on answering the door, but I couldn't do that to him.

I took a deep breath to shake out my nerves and opened the door. Only it wasn't Bishop. Mr. Shepherd stood in front of me in a pair of black slacks, white collared shirt and jacket. His expensive watch gleamed from where it peeked from his sleeve and his mix of salt and pepper hair was smoothed back.

I stiffened. "Can I help you?"

"I sure hope so." He lifted a check book and pen, posed to write. "What's it going to take to get you to back off?"

My jaw dropped. "Excuse me?"

"Listen, I know your type so stop playing coy. You aren't the first and probably won't be the last. That boy is going to give me problems for years, I'm sure. Give me a number."

"He was right about you. Only, you're worse than I thought." I ran my eyes over his posh exterior that hid the vileness on the inside. "I'm not that kind of guy. You can't buy me."

"Fine." His expression hardened. "If the number is that steep then just spit it out. I need to get back to the house for a video conference and I'm already late."

"Goodbye, Mr. Shepherd." I closed the door softly. No way would I tell him Bishop and I had just officially split.

His muffled voice came through the door. "When you change your mind, call me." A card was slipped beneath the door with his contact information.

I snatched it up and tore it into tiny unrecognizable pieces and tossed them in the trash. What was wrong with him? I couldn't believe that'd just happened. The lengths he was willing to go to get rid of me were astonishing despite already knowing how awful he was.

I collapsed on the edge of my bed and lowered onto my back.

"What a fucking asshole," I whispered to myself.

The guy was insane and Bishop's life was going to be miserable with him. And I couldn't do a thing about it. But I certainly wouldn't be fucking paid off.

I wasn't sure if I should tell Bishop his dad had pulled that shit. Would it mess with his head even more? I didn't want to be responsible for that, but didn't he deserve the truth? And what the hell did his dad mean by *You aren't the first*?

# TWELVE
## BISHOP

"FRIENDS," I muttered under my breath. He wanted to be *friends*. Going back to that status was wrong, and it would never work.

Because I loved him.

I'd roamed campus for an hour, wandered down every path and even passed Shaw's dorm once. I'd said I wouldn't cave to the irrational ultimatum my dad had thrown at my feet and had still let him walk away. *What is wrong with me?*

I understood Shaw's decision to break things off. How could I not? It was selfish to ask him to stay by my side, forced to deal with the ongoing battle between my heart and my head when I had the power to put an end to it. And it killed me the way he'd left things. If we were on opposite sides of the situation, I don't know that I could have been the one to end things. His reasoning was heartfelt and came from a good place and that made it worse. It was my turn to prove to him how much I cared and show him that I'd made a mistake to let him think I doubted us. My heart was already sure of the only choice I could live with and watching him walk away cemented my decision.

The struggle had never been between the company and Shaw. At its core, my entire issue had been with giving up on a dream I'd shared with my mom that was never to be. It was time to let it go.

My mom wouldn't want this for me. Wealth wasn't going to make me happy, and my grandmother had provided an inheritance that was more than enough for a comfortable life. The more my thoughts raced around the idea, the deeper my understanding grew.

Simply put, I'd chosen him when I'd let him into my life. He'd believed I was worth the effort when he had every reason to leave me alone, to live in the isolated world I'd built for myself. The strength of our connection was undeniable, and I'd be stupid not to do everything I could to keep him in my life. Forever, if he allowed it. We were young, and maybe forever sounded premature, but to me it wasn't nearly long enough. Life without Shaw was unthinkable and heartbreaking.

My future was uncertain because I had no backup plan. What I'd do after graduation, I had no idea. But I'd made up my mind and was leaving the entertainment business. My dad could fuck off. And as soon as I told him, I was going after Shaw and hope like hell he'd take me back.

Even in the most devastating scenario, where he told me I'd messed up too bad over and over, it was still the right call. My eyes were open.

The bricks, metal and bright lights that made up the clubs weren't the only ties to my mother. Memories of smiles, hugs, holidays, vacations, birthday parties, bedtime stories—all the things that make a childhood—were the real things that bonded me to her. And no one, especially not my dad, could rob me of those.

Although certain about my decision, the massive changes in my life that had occurred only a short ago, caused anxiety to wreak havoc on my nervous system. My arms were shaking, legs trembling, and driving safely was so deeply ingrained there was no way I was getting behind the wheel, so I set off on foot. Taking the main road, I jogged along sidewalks, trekked through residential areas before reaching the long tree-lined lane that led to my father's home. The five mile walk seemed to take an eternity. Too much time to obsess about what I'd say to him. So when I stepped onto his driveway, I had nothing but a jumble of words and no real plan.

The three-tiered fountain came into view as I approached the house. I climbed the steps to the porch, which had so many good and bad memories attached to it, and stopped for a deep breath at the front door I'd be walking into for the last time. Because when I left this time, I wasn't coming back.

I entered the house without knocking and headed straight for the office. When I stepped into the room, I found my dad standing in front of the window, giving me his profile. His posture was slumped and his eyes were glued to a picture frame he held. His fingers caressed the glass. I hadn't seen the frame in a very long time but I remembered it well. It used to be displayed prominently in his office. My mom and dad on their wedding day. She in her gown and he in his tux as they danced. Her smile was bright and she laughed. His eyes lit up as he watched her.

"Why didn't you ever love me like that?" I asked.

He didn't startle. He stayed where he was and continued staring at the photo.

"She loved you more than me. I didn't want kids but did want an heir." He straightened and walked back to his desk, opening a drawer in his desk and sliding the frame into it. He sat in his chair and met my eyes. "I knew she'd be attached to a baby, and when she did conceive, a part of me was excited. A small part. But the moment you came into the world her heart shifted gears and it was yours."

I crossed my arms over my chest and tilted my head. "Your ego couldn't take the hit? She couldn't love us both?"

"She did love me. Not as much as I loved her, though, you see. You were a fussy baby and took up so much of her time." He eyed me with accusation.

"You didn't love me because Mom did," I clarified.

"You stole her away. Night and day. I hardly ever saw her anymore. I don't know why you couldn't just be an easy baby. But you were a boy, so that's what I got out of the deal." His eyes hardened.

I clenched my jaw. He couldn't hurt me because he meant nothing to me. "We need to talk."

"I already know why you're here." He crossed his ankle onto his knee and tapped the armrest.

"And how's that?"

"I'm not stupid, boy. You love him, as I did your mom. I hoped that you or he would change your minds. But I understand real love. Nothing could ever have come between me and your mom. I lucked out falling head over heels for a woman who suited me. It's a shame it didn't happen for you."

"Always the disappointment." I smiled because...fuck him.

He didn't argue. "I paid him a visit earlier today."

"Who? Shaw?" I stepped farther into the office. "What the hell did you say to him?"

He cocked a brow. "I offered him the same deal I did that other kid. He refused so I told him to call me when he changes his mind."

"What is wrong with you?" I exploded. My entire body shook and I was running on pure adrenaline. "Seriously, what the fuck is wrong with you? Do you actually not know how crazy you are?"

He glanced at the drawer where he'd stowed my mom's photo. "He's not going to call."

"Of course he's not going to! I tried to tell you Shaw isn't like that. Jesus, I need to talk to him." I took a step back toward the door. "And I'm out. All of it, I'm done."

"The offer expires the moment you walk out of here." His voice remained calm but his eyes were sharp.

I laughed. "Fuck your offer. It was a prison sentence."

He didn't seem surprised. "I have something for you." He stood casually and walked over to a door that opened to a large closet. One I'd been forbidden to enter. When the door swung open, my jaw dropped. Frames on top of frames neatly stacked on shelves. He slid one from the top and walked toward me holding it out. "Here."

I grabbed it from him and glanced down at the five-by-seven photo. My mom and me. She sat on the front steps of the house with me sitting beside her. I must have been around two, my short legs not even reaching the next step. I was hugged to her side with a big cheesy grin—a matching one to hers.

I gulped, tears welling up in my eyes for the first time in years. I swiped at my face to keep them from falling. "Why are you giving me this?"

He shrugged. "You should have had it long ago. I can't give you what you want. But this belongs to you."

"You've had no problems taking other things that belong to me." I glared and clutched the frame tight.

"Bishop"—he rubbed his eyes—"I know you don't understand and the problem is that I don't either. What you're doing isn't right. I just can't tolerate the thought of you and that boy owning my company one day."

"So you're admitting it's not just the money. It's because I'm gay." My heart hardened further until it was completely closed off. He was no one to me. Just a sperm donor.

He stared at me again and blinked. "It's not right," he repeated.

He'd never been religious. It was just garden variety bigotry and homophobia. And exactly what I'd expected from someone like him.

"This is goodbye," I stated and turned for the door for the last time.

"Yes, I suppose it is." I felt his eyes on me as I walked away, holding the only real gift he'd ever given me.

## THIRTEEN
## SHAW

*"STOP IGNORING MY CALLS."*

*"If you don't respond, I'm coming over."*

*"Meet me for coffee. Just one. I have one more thing to say to you and you can walk away if you still want to after you hear me out."*

I sat at my desk and stared at the screen with a horrible sense of déjà vu. These had undoubtedly been the worst few days of my life. I clutched the phone tight as my fingers hovered over the keyboard. Just one coffee and I could tell him about his dad's attempt to buy me off. Could I handle that? I chewed on my lip before taking the plunge

*"When and where."*

His response was instant. *"Can you come now? I'm already sitting at the café across from campus. I was hoping you'd say yes."*

My stomach clenched. I had expected to have more warning. *"Okay, one coffee. Give me twenty minutes."*

*"I'll wait however long it takes."*

I closed my eyes and set my phone on the desktop. After taking a few calming breaths, I stood and stepped into the bathroom. I caught sight of my reflection and groaned. The last several days hadn't been kind to my appearance and the shadows beneath my eyes had darkened.

A quick shower and shave later, I looked a little better and definitely smelled better. I dressed in a pair of cargo shorts, a soft hunter-green t-shirt and tossed on a ball cap before I stepped into a pair of tennis shoes. I slipped my phone into my pocket and grabbed my keys. Before I stepped into the hall, I took a moment to prepare myself for seeing him a day after leaving him pleading in the park. It was too soon and the wound too fresh. But I had to do this.

The café was only a short walk from my dorm. He was waiting at an outdoor table under the shading of a black and gold canopy. The rich smell of fresh-brewed coffee and pastries permeated the air and my stomach rumbled. He stood up as I approached.

"Hey," I said and took a seat across from him. The chair scraped across the cement as I pulled it closer to the metal bistro style table.

Bishop stared down at me before taking his seat. He looked good, but then he always did to me. His eyes, however, showed the same signs of stress and sleep deprived nights as mine.

"Thanks for coming," he began. He stared.

I cleared my throat. "One cup of coffee...and maybe a bagel."

He slid me a cup of piping hot coffee, which I didn't usually drink, but this morning it sounded perfect. "Here."

I accepted it gratefully and took a sip. "What did you..."

"Hold on, I'll be right back." He stood and went into the bakery, leaving me figuratively scratching my head.

He returned two minutes later holding a striped black and gold paper bag and passed it to me.

"What's this?" I took the bag and opened it. The smell of the warm cinnamon bagel made my stomach growl.

He frowned. "You said you wanted one. If you don't..."

"Oh, no, I definitely do." I pulled out my wallet and dug around for a few dollars."

"Stop, Shaw."

"You can't pay for my things anymore."

He growled. "Yes, I can."

I sighed. "Thank you." I picked off a piece and threw it in my mouth. I groaned as I chewed. "So good."

When I glanced back at him, his eyes were narrowed and his jaw clenched. Last week he would have had me in bed within minutes of that look.

I set the paper bag aside and dusted the crumbs from my fingers. "What did you want to talk about?"

"Right into it, huh?" He rubbed his hands on his shorts. "Okay, my dad said he visited you."

My jaw dropped. "Yeah, after I got home yesterday. He asked me to name a price to stay away from you." I tapped my finger on the table. I was still insulted. "I was actually going to tell you today."

He rubbed his eyes and sighed. "I'm sorry. He doesn't know how to be a decent human being."

"He said I wasn't the first. What the hell does that mean?"

"It means that back in high school he did the same thing, but it worked and the guy took the money."

"He paid off your high school boyfriend?" I felt vaguely nauseous. It was hard for me to picture Bishop dating in high school.

"Nah, he wasn't my boyfriend, but...you know." His cheeks pinked.

My eyebrow rose. "Right, so go on."

"My dad paid him to stay away from me. I thought he'd just run scared after almost getting busted. I wasn't heart-broken or anything so I didn't dig too deep or I might have known." He shrugged.

My jaw dropped. "He took the money?"

He took a sip of his coffee. "Yup. So, I'm sorry I didn't prepare you, but I just found out about it the other day when the whole engagement debacle came up. I was focused on getting out of that and it didn't cross my mind that he'd approach you until he told me yesterday what he had done."

"I'm surprised he told you."

He nodded. "That makes two of us."

"It just caught me off guard." I looked him in the eyes. "I'd *never* take his money. That's fucked up."

"I know you wouldn't. That's probably why I never registered it as a concern or thought to warn you, but I guess he was right in some ways. Some people are after money but not everyone is you."

I swallowed hard. "So you wanted to talk."

He nodded but fidgeted with cup, rolling it from one hand to the other as steam escaped the lid. "This is going to sound crazy, but would you do it? Give it up, I mean. Walk away from it all."

I frowned. "What do you mean?"

"If you were in my position, would you walk away from that future to be with me?" His dark eyes were downcast before flicking back up.

My heart began racing in my chest and the stirrings of a panic attack rode my heels. "You didn't"—I paused—"did you?"

He scowled. "You aren't answering the question."

"And I'm not going to. I can't ask you to do that and I'm

not in that position so I can't understand. It's not a fair question." I was ready to jump and run.

"You didn't ask me to." He held my gaze.

I gaped at him. "You already did it, didn't you?"

He slowly nodded. My world tilted for a moment and I blinked away the stupid mist in my eyes.

"You're insane," I whispered. "That's a pretty steep price to pay to be with me."

"Nothing is worth losing you." My eyes were held by his stare, flames dancing, with deep and powerful emotion. "And I'd pay much more. Everything I have. Totally worth it."

My throat constricted and my jaw clenched as I pushed back down the emotion rising hard and fast. "What about your mom?"

He smiled wistfully. "I think my mom would be pretty damn happy about this. She really loved me and wanted me to be happy above everything else, you know? I was holding on too tight to something that wasn't really there. I thought if I let go, I'd be letting go of our dream, hers and mine. Letting her down somehow. But that dream died the day she did. I didn't care about the company and I have new dreams."

"And they include me?" This was not how I imagined this conversation would go and my stomach was *not* filled with butterflies. Insane bats were trapped in there.

"Shaw, I would have been miserable working with my dad, and the thought of losing you was tearing me apart." He shook his head and smiled. "Wasn't an option and I'm one hundred percent sure my mom approves. She would have loved you. You two have the same optimistic spirit."

I swallowed the lump in my throat and whispered.

"Careful, Shepherd, you sound like you might actually care about me."

His lips twitched before he stood and dragged his chair next to mine. My eyes stayed glued to his as he pressed his knees to mine and leaned in. "I'll one up you, Wakefield." The fucker paused for dramatic effect.

"Oh my god, put me out of my misery." If he didn't stop, I would be the one to spank his ass. Well, maybe not.

He wore a small smile as he grabbed my hands in his and placed them where our knees touched, weaving our fingers together. "Shaw, I'm in love with you."

My breathing stopped as I processed his words. Bishop loved me. I was fairly certain he'd developed feelings, but to hear him call it love, out loud...calmness overcame me as I soaked it in. Things clicked into place and pieces I'd lost over the last few days came back together.

"I wouldn't take it back even if I could, but don't leave me hanging." Bishop spoke and I realized I'd been thinking, but not talking out loud.

My smile was wide and goofy and I didn't care. "I love you, too. So much."

"Yeah?" His face seemed to grow younger with boyish happiness. His mouth spread into a crooked smile and small crinkles appeared at the corners of his eyes.

I reached forward and swept his hair back from his forehead, revealing that small faded scar. "Definitely."

"This is killing me. Can I kiss you yet?" He was already reaching for me.

"I can't believe—" My words were cut off when he darted forward and pressed his lips to mine. His hand went to the back of my head and tangled in my hair as he kissed me senseless. And then kissed me more.

When I broke away, my breathing was ragged as he

rested his forehead on mine. I remembered our surroundings and pulled back.

My gaze fell to my lap. "I don't want to ruin the moment, but I want to make sure this is really it."

"Hey, look at me." He brought his hand to my face, tipping my chin until I met his eyes before he pulled his hand back. "No matter what it is, you and me, we're solid."

I nodded. "Okay, what about your dad and Mya's family? Are they going to be in our lives?"

"They tried to steal my life with you and made us miserable, so no, they won't."

"Thank fuck."

Bishop chuckled.

"So, we're really going to do this? As what? Like a couple...public and all that?" Asking the question was hard because it was something I really wanted.

"If you want me, then you have me."

"I mean, I guess that would be okay." I bit my lip to keep from smiling.

He smirked. "Already asking for the first official boyfriend spanking?"

"Never."

"Liar." A grin split his face, pearly white teeth gleaming, and I could only stare. When Bishop smiled...everything. Just everything. No words.

But another thought struck me and my eyes widened. "What are you going to do for school? Your house and car. Oh, no, are you seriously losing everything?"

"Hey, calm down." He grabbed my hands and held them on my knees again. "I'm okay. *We're* okay. The house was my grandmother's on my mom's side. It's in my name. The car too. I have more than enough in trusts. We don't need him."

"*We*. I like the sound of that," I admitted. I think the shock was starting to wear off and I glanced around. A few people snuck peeks but I didn't care and he didn't seem to either.

I glanced back at him. "What are you going to do now when you graduate?"

"I was just thinking about this yesterday, when I decided I was done with that hot mess. And the answer is I have no idea." He gave me a sheepish grin. "But I guess I better figure it out, huh?"

"Probably a good idea." I chuckled.

"Maybe I'll be a teacher," he suggested.

We both started laughing at the same time. "Oh, those poor kids."

"You don't think I'd make a good teacher?" he teased.

"Not until you learn to stop glaring at everyone." I gave him a pointed look and we both laughed. "You have time to figure it out. You don't need to have all the answers right now."

"Well in the meantime... want to get out of here?"

I sighed as if I was totally put out. "I guess you'd better take me home."

His lip quirked up on one side as he stood. "With pleasure."

He took my hand, yanked me from my seat and walked with me to his car. He took me home, we got naked, crawled into bed together...and then the fucker lay with me wrapped tight, refusing all my advances.

He sighed and buried his face in my neck. "Can we get the rest of your shit and move it in with mine?"

"Convenience?" I asked with a grin though he couldn't see me.

He lifted up onto his elbow and looked down at me. "You know that's not it."

I ran a finger over his jaw, slightly dipping into the cleft in his chin I loved. "I'd be okay with that."

He collapsed again, retaking his place and squeezed me tighter. "Good."

It was mid-morning, but the emotional rollercoaster I'd been through left me exhausted. And I fell asleep with a smile on my face.

# EPILOGUE

## SHAW

"WE COULD HAVE DONE this without Nash," I whispered to Bishop.

Nash's new gunmetal-gray truck was backed into my parents' driveway and we were loading it with Rendon's belongings.

"Yeah, but this was easier than using a rental and he offered." He spoke low since Nash was on the other side of the truck grabbing tie-downs.

When I told my brother over the phone that Nash would help, he'd seemed fine with it, but as soon as they were in the same space it became clear there was tension between them. My brother didn't seem happy to see him.

"Did you see the way Rendon just ignored him?" I wondered if Nash had told my brother they'd been found out. No one had addressed the issue since I called Nash out on it months ago and whatever they'd had going appeared to have ended on bad terms. That was the only thing I could make of Rendon's behavior.

"Stop getting into their business." Bishop gave me a

peck on the cheek. "I know it's hard, but your brother is in college now. He needs to figure out some things for himself."

"I know, but I promised my parents..." How was I supposed to look after him and stay out of his business at the same time? Senior year was going to be rough.

"It's your parents' job to worry. You don't need to hover over him or anything. Just be there for him. He's a big boy now." Bishop patted my head and I sighed.

Rendon stepped out of my parents' small brick home holding a large cardboard box. His scrawny arms struggled to hold onto it and he strained beneath its weight. "This is the last of it."

Nash hurried over to him and relieved him of the box. "Holy shit, Ren, this weighs a ton. What do you have in here?"

"Books." He shoved his black wire glasses up his nose. "And don't call me *Ren*."

Nash carried the box to the bed of his truck and slid it in with the rest of my brother's belongings and he and Bishop began securing everything with the cords he'd brought.

I turned to my brother. "Are you excited about the move?"

He wrinkled his nose and brushed his blond hair from his forehead. "Yeah, I guess."

"You guess? I thought you'd be happier, brainiac."

"I am." He looked over at Nash. "I just have a lot on my mind."

The clang of the tailgate shutting grabbed my attention. "We'd better say bye to Mom and Dad." I bumped his shoulder. "Get ready for the water works."

"I heard that." My mom stepped out of the house in a

flowy, yellow summer dress that brushed her ankles, hair piled on top of her head in a bun and mascara smudge marks beneath her eyes. "You boys don't understand now, but maybe one day you will. When you two drive off today, I'll officially have an empty nest for the first time in over two decades. It's a big deal."

"I'll drive down and visit," Rendon promised.

"And you know I do when I can." I pulled her thin frame into a hug and squeezed her tight. "One more year and then I'll visit so often you'll beg me to go home."

She sniffed and squeezed back. "Never ever."

I chuckled and released her.

"Give me a hug," she told Rendon and he wrapped her in his arms. He wasn't much taller than her, and I towered over them both.

"Mrs. Wakefield." Bishop stepped next to me and nodded at her with a small smile.

"Stop with that Mrs. Wakefield stuff." She smiled. "One day I hope you'll call me Sarah."

I'd brought him home for a day shortly after we'd made things official.

My mother had been thrilled. *Oh, honey, the way he looks at you. He's a good one.* She was sold.

Dad kept giving him the side-eye but when Bishop had taken him outside to check out his ride, they'd become fast friends. My dad had been in awe and Bishop let him take his car for a drive.

"What am I missing out on here?" My dad's gruff voice came from the doorway. His gray hair was brushed down for once and his blue eyes scanned each of us. "Are you boys about ready to leave?"

"We just loaded the last box," Rendon answered.

My dad walked over to us and placed his hand on my brother's shoulder. "Be careful out there and let your brother know if you need anything at all."

"I will, I promise." He gave him a quick hug and crossed the lawn to his small car parked at the curb. He opened the door and with a bright smile, waved back at my mom before hopping in.

I patted Dad's back. "He'll be all right. Looks like you're going to have your hands full." I tipped my chin in my mother's direction.

He followed my gaze to my mom who had her arms hugged around her body.

"She'll be okay. It's tough on her, but she's super proud of both of you. We both are. She goes on and on about you two to her friends." He ruffled my hair. "The season starts up soon so we will be visiting quite a bit anyway."

"All right, well, we need to get on the road. I love you guys."

"Love you too, kiddo." My dad gave me a quick side hug.

I pecked my mom's cheek and she beamed. "Bye, sweet boy."

I chuckled. "Bye, Mom."

Everyone said their goodbyes and then the three of us climbed in the truck. I took the backseat and we pulled away, I glanced back and saw my dad with an arm around my mom who had her face buried in his shirt. They turned and walked into the house.

We followed behind Rendon's little car out of town and back to Sugar Land where we pulled into the same parking lot I'd used when I'd lived on campus. My brother had been assigned a room in the same building.

Rendon got out of his car and loaded up with an arm full of bedding. He headed for the entrance and Nash rolled down his window. "Hey, what room are we looking for?"

Rendon called out a number I couldn't hear, but Nash nodded. We piled out of the truck and circled to the bed as Nash lowered the tailgate. We each grabbed a box.

I glanced over at Bishop as we ambled up the path to the entrance, remembering the times I had sat in my room before I'd made the permanent move to Bishop's.

He caught me looking and his lips twitched. "I love you even when you're being creepy and staring at me."

Both Nash and I snorted.

"I love you back." When he glanced at me with heat in his eyes, I bit my lip.

"That shit is still weird." Nash pretended to gag over his shoulder as we entered the building.

"You're welcome to mind your own business," Bishop growled.

I adjusted the box in my arms and chuckled. As we began climbing steps, I glanced over my shoulder and smirked at my boyfriend. "He's just jealous."

"Nah." Nash shook his head. "You know me. That's not my thing. You two are just disgustingly happy."

"Fuck you." I laughed.

"Nah, you're not my type, and even if you were, Bishop's ass would kill me."

Bishop was silent as he followed behind me down the hallway, but I could picture him drilling a hole in the back of Nash's head with a glare.

Rendon stepped out of his new room and waved us in, but paused when he saw Nash was first. He was quick to look away and turned to go back into the room. There wasn't a question in my mind something had happened between them. Nash may as well have confirmed it when I'd called him out on it months ago. I was still peeved at my friend.

"Where do you want me?" Nash asked Rendon with a hint of suggestion that made my skin crawl.

Rendon's gaze snapped back to Nash and his eyes narrowed. "The *boxes* can go on the floor over there."

Nash chuckled before unloading the box by the desk.

"You ready for this?" I asked my brother, after I set my own load next to the other one.

He nodded. "Yeah, I think so."

Bishop stepped around and silently put the third one on top of mine.

"Let's go grab the rest, guys," I said.

We made two more trips until his half of the room was a mess for him to unpack. He was on his own with that.

"All set?" I asked Rendon.

"Yup, thank you guys for helping me," he said to me and Bishop. Reluctantly he turned to Nash. "Thanks for offering to use your truck. It made things a lot easier."

Nash grinned. "No problem, Ren."

"My name is Ren*don*." He pursed his lips.

"All right," I broke up the argument. "You two can fight about your name another time. Call if you need anything at all. Our house isn't far and I can be here in ten minutes flat."

"I know. You've told me, like a million times." He blew his shaggy blond bangs up, which then were sent fluttering right back down over his green eyes behind his glasses.

I pulled my phone from my pocket and checked the time. "We gotta run if we want to make it to the center on time." We were due to study some film and would have our asses handed to us if we were late.

"Better you than me," Rendon muttered as he opened the first box and began unpacking his clothes.

"We have a championship to win this year!" Nash hooted. "Gotta be ready."

"So you told me." Rendon dropped the verbal bomb and everyone froze. It was the first time either of them admitted out loud they had a history, so any doubt I may have had, which was slim at most, was squashed.

Nash let out a nervous chuckle and turned toward me. We held a stare off, his eyes shifting and mine narrowed.

"So practice?" he asked and averted his eyes to the wall behind me. "Yep, we're going to be late. Better hurry."

He cast Rendon one more glance before walking from the room.

I stayed behind with Bishop and cleared my throat. "Rendon—"

He held up a hand. "Don't start lecturing me. I know what I'm doing."

I glanced at Bishop for help, so he sighed and stepped forward. "Be careful with Nash."

"Why?" Rendon's nose wrinkled.

"He doesn't take relationships seriously. I don't think he's ever even dated. Hookups..." Bishop trailed off when Rendon crossed his arms and his expression hardened.

He was so young and Nash, while a great guy at heart, just hadn't ever expressed interest in anyone in an exclusive way. I'd never even seen him with anyone outside of a party or club.

"Thanks for the advice." My brother's tone suggested he was calm and cool, but the slight wobble in his voice led me to believe otherwise. "I know what Nash is like, so there's nothing to worry about."

Of course, I'd worry anyway. He was in college now and in control of his own life. What could I really do? I didn't need issues with my teammate, but if he hurt Rendon, there would be problems between us.

I reluctantly left with Bishop, but once we'd reached the bottom floor, I tugged on Bishop's arm.

He stopped and turned to me. "What's wrong?"

"I'm definitely concerned."

He hummed and reached for me, pulling me into his arms. "This is going to drive you crazy, but you really do have to step aside and let your brother handle their relationship."

I nodded because he was right. That didn't mean I had to like it. "I'm not sure we can call whatever is going on between them a relationship. I mean it's Nash, you know?"

"I get it, but Rendon's in college, preparing for the adult world and new experiences. Sometimes you're just going to have to let him figure it out and just be there for him."

I scrubbed my hands over my face. Why did he have to choose Nash, or rather, why did Nash choose him?

"Hey." He leaned forward and pressed his lips to mine. "It'll all be okay."

He released me and we walked back to the truck. Nash was in the driver's seat messing with his phone when we climbed in.

From the backseat, I glared at him in the rearview mirror. Without looking up, he sighed. "Right, so I might have withheld the truth before, a little. But you should know, I didn't walk away." He paused. "He did."

My eyes jerked to Bishop's, who was already twisted in his seat, and we shared a look.

*What?*

The End

...Almost

Read on for a bonus scene of how Bishop and Shaw started their arrangement.

# BONUS SCENE

## BISHOP

The bands on my arms were soaked with sweat and my body ached as we readied for another down. This could well be the last play of the game and we were only up by one touchdown. Despite how well we'd played, the Ravens had pushed us back into the red zone. I stood ready behind the line of scrimmage, darting forward and backing up, trying to get them to jump before the snap.

"Ready!" The Raven's QB crouched and held his hands toward his center. "Blue Seventeen, Blue Seventeen."

He grunted and all hell broke loose. My eyes stayed on the ball. The QB's eyes focused on the end zone and both of their star wide receivers took off in a run, but I'd studied enough film to know their quarterback's tell. I was ready.

The handoff was subtle and well played. To most, he probably looked like he was still about to throw the ball, but then their smallest player broke through our defense, ball tucked tight against his chest. Small and compact, quick on his feet, he barreled through the bigger players and I sprinted toward him.

I thrived on the slight widening of an opponent's eyes

right before you wrapped their asses up and threw them to the ground. Well, that didn't happen. The little shit spun around and I had to adjust on the fly. I dove and wrapped my hand around his lower leg and he went down hard.

He grunted and both of our gazes whipped up to the clock. He hadn't cleared the first down marker so the clock still ran.

"Fuck." He jumped up and knocked his shoulder pads into mine as he ran back to the line with the ball.

I took my position again, but they weren't quick enough to get the ball snapped and the game ended with the referee blowing the final whistle. The crowd's noise was deafening and you couldn't tell the different between cheers and boos. It was a madhouse.

"Hell, yes!" One of my teammates gripped the back of my pads and shook me.

A few patted my helmet and back as we raced back to the sidelines.

"That's how you do it, boys." Coach Sanders clapped. "Good stop, Bishop!"

I stripped off my black and gold helmet and the chilly wind whipped through my damp hair. Cheers went up around me as the team celebrated. Two of my teammates rushed by and I stepped aside as a giant orange barrel was lifted over Coach, drenching his entire back. He grimaced before laughing. My lips twitched.

The home crowd was still going wild as I stood back and took it all in. Many of these guys were here on a football scholarship. I didn't need one, so I played for the outlet it gave me, to burn off pent-up frustration, largely caused by my dad. He hadn't wanted me to play and I told him I'd only attend Sugar Land, the closest university to home, if I got to play ball. But I didn't do it for the glory or camaraderie afterward, so I observed as others enjoyed it.

My gaze landed on Shaw. Blond hair, green eyes and easy smile, my eyes *always* stopped on Shaw. Something about him drew me to him. He smiled at the others and used the pads of our giant center, Rush, to push on and jump in the air. Crazy bastard.

The field became a chaotic mess of players from both teams, as well as staff, security and reporters. Hands were shaken, quiet insults passed back and forth and photographers pushed through to take photos.

Torin, our quarterback, was grabbed for an interview and another headed my way. I walked away before I had to answer any questions. The only reporter I was interested in talking to hadn't even earned his journalism degree yet. It was a perfect job for a people person like Shaw. As I passed him, his gaze caught mine.

"Nice stop, man!" He turned and joined me as I walked toward the tunnel.

"Thanks."

"Thanks," he mocked with a monotone voice. "Man of many words."

"Shut up." I resisted the urge to smile by biting the inside of my cheek.

He laughed. "There's a party tonight at Beau's house. You coming?"

"I don't go to parties."

"I'm aware of that, my friend. We are all aware of that. But we only have two weekends off every season. Bye week is the only time we can get away with this shit. You have to come."

"Do I?"

"Dude, you can't only talk to me. Some of the guys on the team aren't that bad, I promise."

"So you keep telling me." I'd attempted to keep Shaw at arm's length too but had only lasted a few months before I caved to his relentless attempts to become my friend.

"Buzz kill. You have to come tonight. I'll be lonely without you."

I glanced at him and scoffed when he pretended to pout. "You're never lonely. Isn't one of your girls going to be there?"

"If I said yes, would that bother you?"

My steps slowed. "Why would it bother me?"

Shaw shrugged. "You asked if they were going to be there. If I said no, would you come?"

"If you said no, you'd be a liar." I sped back up.

He chuckled as we entered the locker-room. After a quick shower and change back into our street clothes, we packed up our gear and said goodbyes.

"Hey, Shaw." Beau, our defensive captain, called out as we were about to exit. Shaw paused but I kept going. "You're still coming tonight, right?"

"Yep, I'll see you guys later."

"Sweet. I'd ask Bishop, but you know..." He said it like I wasn't still in hearing distance.

"Oh, I know." Shaw laughed and ran to catch up with me. "The guys think you're weird."

"Why do I care?" I turned in the direction of where I'd parked.

"You don't. I was just saying..." he called out as we parted ways and I glanced back. "Rose Hill Road. You can't miss the cars. I'll be there around eleven and you better come. Don't say no."

He ducked into his older blue sedan before I could

respond. I wasn't actually going to go to the party. Why would I? I didn't drink. I didn't dance. The only reason I would go was to hang out with Shaw, which I probably already did too much since I was attracted to my friend.

---

My house had belonged to my grandparents when I was a kid. As always, now, it was quiet when I got home. The spacious living room was filled with nice furniture that nobody but me used. After I'd whipped up something to eat and settled on the couch, I flipped the TV on to add some damn noise in the house and dug into my late dinner.

Shaw's invitation to the party was in the back of my mind. The guys were okay, but that wasn't a reason to go. I saw them all the time. The more I attempted to convince myself that going was a bad idea, the stronger the urge grew to pick up my phone and tell Shaw he'd won and I'd be there.

I was in my closet and dressing for the damn party before I even fully processed that I'd decided to go. Once in my car, I worried I'd made the wrong call. The guys thought I was weird, Shaw had said, and I didn't want to draw attention to myself. *I don't have to stay if I'm not feeling it.*

I knew the road where they were having the party well enough. It was close to campus and I drove by there every day. When I reached the street, I exhaled hard. He hadn't exaggerated about the cars. The house was lit up and people were everywhere. I didn't expect it to be long before the cops were called, but what did I know? The city worshipped Sugar Land Saints football.

"What the fuck am I doing here?" I said aloud.

There was one empty curbside space several houses

away and I pulled into it. The dashboard clock showed eleven fifteen when I climbed out of my car and set the alarm. As I walked down the sidewalk toward the house, I scanned the cars outside. No sign of Shaw's. I was tempted to pick up my phone and text him to find out if he'd already arrived, but showing up at all was bad enough. He'd know I'd only done it because he'd asked. I wasn't going to fucking text him too.

I wove through the people loitering around the front yard and entered the brown brick house. Black and gold balloons and streamers littered the entrance and every wall in sight. I avoided gazes that swung my way as I edged a path along the walls into the living room. I wasn't claustrophobic, but it was hard not to feel trapped with so many people packed in one room. I found an empty spot against the wall in a corner that hid me from the crowd and scanned the room for Shaw. I came up empty.

"Hey, Bishop!" Beau approached me. "I'm glad you made it. I didn't think you would."

"Me either," I mumbled.

He laughed, showing straight white teeth against pale skin that was dotted in freckles and matched his rust-toned hair. "You planning on staying cooped up over here the whole night? Do you want a beer, man? There's more than enough in the kitchen."

"Nah," I paused. "Thanks though."

"Sure." He took a drink of his own beer. "Is Shaw here yet? I haven't seen him."

Why was he asking me? "Ah, I'm not sure."

"Are you waiting on him?"

My brows furrowed and I lied. "No."

"Okay." He grinned and took a step back. "Well, enjoy the party."

I glanced away, my gaze roaming over faces. Most of my teammates were there, along with people I recognized from school, and some I'd never met.

Nash, a wide receiver like Shaw, caught my eye and waved me over to a group of people he was hanging out with. I shook my head and he headed my way.

"Hey," he said and took the spot along the wall next to me. "You see Shaw?"

"No." Why did everyone keep asking me that?

"Oh, I figured you guys rode together." He pulled a cherry sucker out of his pocket, unwrapped it and popped it into his mouth. The guy had a serious addiction to those things.

"We didn't," I responded. Shaw should have been there already.

Nash rolled his eyes and pulled out his sucker. "Yeah, I got that."

He stood for another moment. "There's some girls wanting to go jump in the pool. Pretty hot, so if you want to call dibs, you better go now."

"I don't."

"Well, as interesting as this conversation has been." His yellow-green eyes flashed with amusement. "I'm going to go...have fun. There's some hot guys out there too." He waggled his brows. Nash was openly bi and I envied his confidence to come out to the team, and everyone else for that matter.

He walked away and I leaned against the wall. If Shaw didn't show up in another five minutes, I was leaving. No use in standing there by myself like a loser.

I stuffed my hand in my pocket and jingled my keys. But then he walked into the room and turned his head side to side as he scanned the room. When his eyes met mine, a smile stretched across his face and he squeezed past people until he stood in front of me.

"Thought you said you weren't coming." He took the spot Nash had vacated and leaned his hip and shoulder against the wall as he faced me. One hand was wrapped around a beer bottle.

"So? Did you bring a girl then?" I didn't know why that was the first question I asked.

He pointed at me and gave me a victorious smile. "I knew it. You totally would leave right now if I did, wouldn't you?"

"Did I say that?" I attempted to backtrack.

I didn't care if he brought a girl, but if he had, he'd disappear with her eventually. I wasn't going to stay and hang out by myself so, yeah, I'd leave.

"Well, if you're not here because of me, then why did you come? You're just standing here like a piece of furniture." He cocked his head to the side.

"Maybe I was curious." That was partly true, I supposed.

"Curious." He took a pull of his beer from the bottle then hummed. "Well, are you?"

"Am I curious?" My brow furrowed. "About what?"

"You said maybe you were curious, so you tell me." He grinned. "This is the weirdest conversation we've ever had and that says something."

I bit back a smile.

"Yeah, I was talking about the party." The lies were practically dripping from my tongue. "I'm horribly let down at how accurate I was in assuming it would be lame."

"You could always find a chick to hook up with." He made a show of looking around. "There are plenty of them here."

I'd never given any of the guys a reason to think I was gay. My hookups were mostly from an app and I never had to see them again, though that was getting old. "Nah, I'm good."

"Then I guess I'm walling it with you." He turned his back to the wall and widened his legs, but he turned his head to face me.

I felt as lame as I'd accused the party of being. "You don't have to."

"I invited you. I'm not going to like leave you here. What kind of friend do you take me for?" He tried to appear hurt, but his grin burst through.

"I told you I only came..." I paused when he lifted a brow. "I'm probably about to leave anyway."

"I just got here." He bumped my shoulder. "It's bad form to abandon your friend at parties you know. Safety in numbers."

"Shut up. You have plenty of friends here, and I'm sure you're more than capable of *handling* yourself with the hordes of women waiting to jump your bones." The thought settled like a brick in my stomach. It was true and there was no way I'd stand around and watch it happen.

He huffed. "What would you rather be doing?"

*You.* The immediate thought wasn't the first time it crossed my mind, but even if Shaw were gay, it'd be a bad decision to fuck a teammate. "I don't know. Probably swimming at my house or relaxing on the couch."

"Boring. There's so many things to *do*." He bit his lip and my gaze fell to his full lips.

"Boring is underrated. There's something simple and comforting about it," I insisted.

"Even more boring." He pretended to yawn and I bumped his shoulder that time.

"Shut up." A raspy chuckle escaped and I clamped my mouth shut. He grinned.

The house filled with more people in a never-ending stream of newcomers and I contemplated calling it a night and heading home. "Is the whole team here?"

"Most of them. I don't think I've seen Rush or Torin." He shrugged. "They rarely show up at these parties."

"What's the deal with those two?" I had wondered about them from our first football season together. The two were always up each other's asses.

"Best friends growing up, I believe. Beyond that is anyone's guess, but there's some speculation that they are together." He lowered his voice in a whisper and made a kissing noise. "Like together, together."

I considered the possibility and it rang with a bit of truth. They were definitely close to each other. "Do you think they are?"

He shrugged. "Don't know. Doesn't make a difference to me. Hold my beer?" He held the mostly-full bottle out to me. "I gotta find the bathroom."

"Uh, sure." I took the beer from him. "I didn't think you drank."

"Not very much or often," he replied. "Be right back."

I tracked his movements as he rounded the stairs and climbed the steps until he disappeared from sight.

A few minutes of people watching later, my phone vibrated against my leg and I pulled it from my pocket.

The preview showed it was from Shaw. I frowned and pulled up the message.

*"Come upstairs for a second."*

I chewed on my lip while I wondered what he needed me for. After a quick glance at my surroundings, I peeled my back from the wall, circled the stairs and followed

Shaw's path. A few people sat side-by-side on a lower step and I excused myself as I passed them, but once I reached the landing, I wasn't sure where to go.

I tapped on my phone's screen. *"Where?"*

A door creaked open and his blond head poked out. "In here."

I walked into the bathroom and he shut the door behind us. "Um, what are you doing?"

He stared at me for a minute and then stepped forward, leaned in to me and kissed me. I froze, until his tongue traced my bottom lip.

I growled and pushed him against the wall. My dick rose, rock hard, trapped between us. "What are you doing, Shaw?"

"I knew it." He pushed his hips into mine.

I tensed. "Knew what?"

"Stop playing stupid. Kiss me. Trust me, I want it."

My eyes narrowed. "Is this a trick?"

"What? Why the fuck would I trick you into kissing me." He rocked into me, letting me feel how hard he was.

Fucking hell.

I searched his eyes for a hint of a lie and I believed him. It was me who instigated the second kiss. I slipped my tongue inside his mouth and he welcomed it with a moan as he greedily grasped the back of my head, holding me to him.

I pulled away. "How did you know?"

"What? That you were gay or maybe bi? Or that you're into me?"

"If you didn't have a dick I wouldn't be doing this." I answered his first question and he ground against me. "And who says I'm into you."

He paused. "Well, are you?"

"I'm not interested in anything serious." Not that that's

what he'd asked, but I felt it was important to address it before I ruined the only friendship I had.

He laughed. "I'm definitely not looking for serious."

Our lips crashed together again and his hand reached between our bodies and undid the button on my pants. I groaned. "Here?"

"Yes."

"Bottom or top?"

He groaned. "Bottom. I want your cock so bad. Have for a while."

My dick throbbed. "Thank fuck."

I snatched his hands from the zipper he was undoing and spun him around toward the sink.

"Do you have a condom and lube?" he asked.

"Yes." I pulled out my wallet and set them on the counter.

He looked at me in the mirror almost accusingly. "Convenient."

"Tonight it seems to be." I raised my brows.

"It is that," he agreed and pushed back against me, grinding his ass against my junk.

"Hands on the counter. Don't move."

His eyes opened wide in surprise and his lids lowered and his mouth parted. "Yes, sir."

"None of that sir shit."

He licked his lips. "Oh, you'll like it, sir."

"You're already a pain in my ass, don't make it worse."

"A little pain, more pleasure in *my* ass, please." His top teeth sank into his lush lower lip.

"Fuck, you're so fucking..." I reached around and unzipped him, pulling his zipper down then yanked his jeans and briefs in one go and let them fall to the floor. "Step out of them."

He did and my gaze dropped to his light tan ass. Muscled and tight. I ran my hands over the smooth skin. "Definitely pleasure."

He lifted his hand, reached back and palmed my cock through my jeans. I pressed against him and then shook my head. I gripped his hand and jerked it back onto the counter. "You don't listen well. Don't move."

A second later my hand landed with a loud slap on his ass and we both froze. The room was filled with silence and heavy breathing. He arched his back and moaned. "Do it again."

I cursed. "You're a bossy little shit. We'll have to fix that."

"Oh, will—"

My hand landed again with a solid smack in a different spot and it immediately turned pink. He moaned louder and I covered his mouth with my hand. He moved his head fast, took one finger in his mouth and bit it.

I hissed and jerked my hand away. "You're asking for it. You want my cock?"

"So damn much." His eyes were molten in the reflection.

"Then do as you're told and stay still."

"Make me," he taunted.

The spank that landed that time was harder and my palm stung.

He gasped but stilled. "Oh my god, fuck me already."

I was suited up and slicked in seconds. I brought my hands to his reddened ass and then squeezed both his warm cheeks, spreading them. I looked down and groaned at the sight of his hole and hanging sac. I released one cheek and grazed my finger over the tight entrance.

"Please stop teasing and stretch me." He shifted his hips and I realized he wasn't capable of staying still for very long.

I loved how I could see every expression that crossed his face when I did different things to him. It was so telling, and his gaze begged for more.

I continued to rub my finger back and forth.

"You're such an ass—" He hissed when I slid a finger inside him and shivered. "Give me more."

I moved in and out, finger fucking him until I felt he was ready for the second. The sounds that escaped his lips were driving me crazy. Once I got to three, he grew even more impatient, fucking himself on my fingers. "You're a horny little shit."

"Complaining?" he asked "And yes, I am, so give it to me already."

I pulled my fingers out then lined up my tip to his hole. Teasing him, I pushed against him with light pressure before retreating. "I'll decide when I'm ready."

"Well, when someone notices us missing because you're taking your sweet time, just remember—"

I thrust inside him, seating myself fully and pressed flush with him.

"Motherfucker. You get off of on surprise attacks?" he asked but his eyes rolled back as he ground against me.

"Complaining?" I threw his word back at him. "You wanted my cock. You got it." I pulled back before driving forward. "And I'm going to fuck you stupid."

His mouth fell open and I devoured his expression in the mirror like the sweetest dessert.

"Harder." He groaned.

"Happily." I slammed into him over and over until my cock ached with the need to come.

"God, yes." He moaned so loud, but I was too far gone to care. "I knew you'd be good."

I smacked his ass which only made him louder.

"Oh shit." He pushed back, fucking me as much as I fucked him. "I'm going to come and I haven't even touched my cock."

"And you won't." I wrapped my hand around his shaft, which was smooth, long and hard and jacked him fast. My balls were drawn tight and the need to come was growing beyond my control. If I was going to blow my load, he'd do it right with me.

He continued taking me deep, meeting me thrust for thrust, fucking himself on me. I imagined him riding me and how he'd look as he bounced on my cock, hips swiveling, dick hard and irresistible. I'd jerk his ass off me, pull him to my face and swallow his dick...

I came. And I came fucking hard. He clamped down around me and warm come coated my hand at the same time. Curses and moans filled the room as wave after wave of aftershocks wracked my body. His muscles continued to spasm, milking me.

As our heart rates slowed down, I rested my forehead on his shoulder.

"Your ass is incredible," I panted.

"I could say the same about how you use your cock." He rocked back and groaned. "Fuck that was damn good."

My dick was still hard and I was tempted to go again, but he'd had a point earlier. We'd been gone too long, so I pulled out and tied off the condom, tossing it in the trash. Shaw was already cleaning himself up with tissues and searching the cabinets for cleaner as I pulled up my pants and fastened them.

"So, yours or mine for round two?" he asked casually as he pulled his jeans up.

I paused and he glanced over at him. "We said nothing serious."

"What's serious about another round?" His brows furrowed. "It was good, right?"

"Like one more time?" I bit my lip and ran my gaze over him, head to toe, because the thought was tempting.

"Or more. We could like make a thing of it. No strings, ya know? Like friends with benefits." He shrugged. "It'd be easier than finding hookups and staying off people's radar. You're obviously not out and neither am I. It makes sense."

Did I want to sign up for that? I pictured all the ways I would have him and they were damn hot, but what if he got the wrong idea? "No strings. Ever."

"That's what I just said." He rolled his eyes. "If I didn't already know what an asshole you were, I might be offended. Between football, classes and everything, I don't have time for any kind of committed relationship. And that suits me just fine."

It would be convenient and I liked Shaw, was attracted as hell to him and we got along. Then I thought about the chicks I'd seen him with. "So are you bisexual?"

"Yeah, everyone at home knows and it wasn't too big of a deal. My family doesn't care but you know, small towns. I hadn't any plans to keep it to myself here, but seeing Nash and Rush catch shit all the time, I just figured better not to announce it."

I'd seen the same, but regardless, I had no intention of coming out anytime soon. Hadn't even considered it. My father would just love another reason to make my life difficult. As if he hadn't ruined my life anyway by taking my mom away from me.

I nodded as I considered his words. But if we were doing this, I wasn't going to share with chicks *or* other guys. The thought was such a turn off. Call me greedy, but those were my terms.

"I don't share." I watched him for an indication that he had an issue with that.

"I wondered how you'd react if I said the same." He tilted his head. "Guess we're on the same page."

"While we do this, no one else," I added for clarity.

"Right, exclusive fuck buddies. That has a nice ring." He nodded like it made all the sense in the world but his words caused me to pause again.

"It sounds an awful lot like a relationship." And it did. Was it a bad idea?

"Nah, not if we don't like fall in love." He snorted.

I chuckled. "No worries there, but I'm offended you don't think you could fall in love with me."

He rolled his eyes. "You're sort of a jerk. But I like you anyway. So it's settled then?" When I nodded still a little wary, he winked. "Then take me home, sir, and fuck my brains out. Maybe I'll even suck you off."

I groaned at the thought of Shaw's tall frame, fully naked, body muscled and toned, on his knees, my cock slipping through his lips over and over as his warm mouth worked me over. If I was being honest, I was dying to taste him too.

"Yes to sucking me off, but stop with the *sir* shit."

"I've never had anyone spank me and boss me around. Turns out, I'm totally into it. I was fucking around calling you sir, but you know I'll do it just to rile you up now, right?"

"Then I'll spank your ass until you can't take it anymore."

"Promises, promises." He went to fasten his own pants, but I grabbed his shoulders.

I spun him around. With his pants still around loose on his hips, I easily shoved them down.

"Fuck you can't even wait until we get out of here?"

"No," I said and smacked his ass hard.

He pushed back. "More."

I brought my hand down harder. "You *do* like it rough, huh?"

"Take me home and let's find out."

I backed away and adjusted my cock in my jeans. No need to give anyone else an eyeful. "Get dressed, we're leaving."

**The End**

## ABOUT BAYLIN

Bios are challenging. I don't have a clue how to write about myself. Fictional characters? Sure! Me? Not so much. It's the reason my author bio stayed practically blank until after I finished my second novel.

Who am I? Well, I guess I should start by telling you that I write MM romance and I love what I do.

I fell in love with writing during elementary school with my first "Bare Book" but honestly never thought I'd become an author. It always seemed to be something I dreamed of and not something I could make a reality. Now that I have, I can't picture myself doing anything else.

I live in Texas where the heat and I don't get along. One day I hope to call Northeast USA home. I'm a mother of two ridiculously cute kids. I have two dogs and one cat, the latter of which is a spoiled brat, but she's my spoiled brat.

Spending the day under a fluffy blanket reading or writing away on my laptop with a mountain of coffee is my idea of time well spent. I get to live so many lives through books that I consider myself genuinely lucky to call myself an avid reader. Books, whether I'm reading or writing them, make up a huge part of my life and I wouldn't have it any other way.

# ACKNOWLEDGMENTS

This book wouldn't have been published without my incredibly appreciated support team.

Kid one and two, you better never actually be reading this. You two rock for understanding and finding ways to keep busy while I was stationed in front of my laptop for hours on end.

To my loudest cheerleader, my mom, you are probably the biggest reason my books see the light of day. Thank you for all your pep talks and all-around support.

Kathy, you know I couldn't do this without you. Thank you for everything you do.

My Crow's Clubhouse reader group, you all are amazing. It's nice to know I've got my own corner of the online world filled with readers and authors who support my work and provide a positive and fun atmosphere.

Thank you to the many authors, groups and blogs that help spread the word of Broken Play.

To you, the reader, I couldn't do this whole author thing without you. Thank you for reading, reviewing, recommending and sharing the book. It means the absolute world to me.

XOXO -Baylin

Made in the USA
Columbia, SC
12 May 2022